A VISION

Before Julia could figure out how she was supposed to get back inside her body, her vision strayed to the moonlight on the surface of the pond. In fact, her vision moved in that direction quite deliberately, in spite of the memory of her mother's warning —or maybe because of it. She had always been curious as to what she would see in the cool white light.

Now she was trapped.

The trap was similar to when she'd accidentally stumbled upon the execution of the Chinese students. She could probably have broken it with a supreme exercise of will. Yet something about the scene held her fascinated, in a sick sort of way. It was not a typical viewing. It was as if the pond had filled with gray smoke, or as if the place she had stumbled onto was cloaked in thick fog. The images were jumbled. There was a liquor store. There was a young man in a jacket. There was a girl. There was another guy. He was holding something black and hard.

It was a gun.

CHRISTOPHER PIKE

WITCH

POCKET PULSE

New York   London   Toronto   Sydney   Singapore

For information regarding special discounts for bulk purchases,
please contact Simon & Schuster Special Sales at 1-800-456-6798
or business@simonandschuster.com

This book is a work of fiction. Names, characters, places and
incidents are products of the author's imagination or are used
fictitiously. Any resemblance to actual events or locales or persons,
living or dead, is entirely coincidental.

POCKET PULSE published by
Pocket Books, a division of Simon & Schuster, Inc.
1230 Avenue of the Americas, New York, NY 10020

Copyright © 1990 by Christopher Pike

Originally published in 1990 by Archway Paperbacks

ISBN: 0-7434-2799-8

First Pocket Pulse printing September 2001

10 9 8 7 6 5 4 3 2 1

POCKET PULSE and colophon are trademarks of
Simon & Schuster, Inc.

Front cover illustration by David Stevenson
Front cover photos by Tony Stone Images

Printed in the U.S.A.

For Ann

WITCH

Chapter One

JULIA Florence didn't think of herself as a witch. She didn't ride a broom. She didn't cast spells. She didn't even own a cat. But she had abilities few seventeen-year-old girls had. She could heal those who were sick. She could also see what was happening in distant places. There was even a time she saw the future.

It happened at the beginning of her senior year in high school. It was a Friday. The first week of school had just ended, and the first football game was only a couple of hours from starting. Julia was at home, wondering if she should go. The entire summer she had stayed close to home, except when she hiked alone in the quiet woods that stretched for miles beyond her back door. The lush forests were interrupted only by sparkling streams and fields. Julia lived in northern Idaho, two miles outside a modest-size town named Indian Pole. The area had been home to her for her entire life.

Indian Pole High was her alma mater. It had an

1

imposing totem pole in its courtyard, of course—and a dismal football team. Deciding whether to attend the game, Julia asked herself if she needed to see her school lose once again. She knew they would lose, and not because she was a witch. They had lost *every* game the year before. They weren't a big school and didn't have a large pool of football talent. Word was that this would be their weakest team ever.

But Julia loved football. She loved all sports. The reason she was hesitating to attend the game, she realized with a start, had nothing to do with the team's win-lose record. She was feeling sorry for herself again. She didn't want to go to the game because her mother couldn't accompany her as she had before. Her mom had died three months earlier, the same day school had let out for the summer.

Julia still wasn't over it. She knew she never would be. Her mom had been the most wonderful person in the world. She had also been a powerful witch. She was one of the few people on earth who understood Julia's gifts. But those gifts, Julia thought bitterly, had been of no use to save her mom.

Julia felt terribly lonely. Yet she chose to be alone. She was afraid to see other people, to let the hurt go. She was afraid that if she did, the memories of her mother would also go. They would fade and become like the ash of her mother's remains, to be lost on the wind.

The phone rang. It rang and rang. Julia waited a full minute before answering it, deciding if she wanted to. It was her best friend, Amy Belle. Julia had seen Amy at the most twice all summer.

"How are you?" Amy asked.

2

"Great," Julia said. "How are you? What's up?"

"Are you going to the game?"

"I don't know."

"Julia!"

"We're just going to lose."

"You said you'd go," Amy said.

"I didn't say that."

"Liar! Scott is standing right here. Did Julia say she was going to the game? Scott says you swore you'd be there. What kind of person are you? You lie to your friends. Scott is crying now. He says he's going to slit his wrists if you don't come. He's picking up a knife. God, he's sharpening it! You've got to come. We're playing Saddleback tonight. You'll get to meet Jim."

Scott Hague was a long-time buddy of both Julia and Amy. Jim Kovic was Amy's new boyfriend. Julia had heard only good things about Jim. He played fullback for Saddleback High. Julia was glad that Amy had finally met someone she could really care about. Amy deserved to be happy, Julia thought.

"Where's Jim now?" Julia asked. "Is he there?"

"No." Amy laughed. "Is he with you?"

It was an old joke that Julia always stole Amy's boyfriends. At least Julia thought it was a joke. Several of Amy's boyfriends had called Julia up and asked her out. It wouldn't have been so bad, except they were still going with Amy at the time. Julia had told them all no. She didn't understand why so many guys wanted her.

"I'm in the kitchen," Julia said. "He might be in my bedroom."

"Then tell him to get out," Amy said. "He's half Saddleback's offense. Seriously, you have to come.

Scott and I insist. He's still sharpening his knife. He misses you. We'll pick you up. We're on our way. Bye!"

"Wait! The game doesn't start for a couple of hours."

"Then we'll have good seats," Amy said. "Come on, say yes."

Julia sighed to herself. "Yes."

"Great! We're on our way."

"No," Julia said firmly. "I'll meet you there."

"Why don't you come with us?" Amy asked.

"I have some things to do first. Don't worry about me."

Amy lowered her voice. "I do worry about you, Julia. You know that."

Julia was touched. "I know. But don't. Please? I'm OK. I'll see you soon. I promise. Tell Scott I swear it in blood."

Amy believed her. They exchanged goodbyes. Julia set down the phone and looked out the back window. There was plenty of daylight left. She decided to go for a walk. She thought she might visit the pond.

There was a chill in the air, but Julia didn't bring a sweater or coat to cover her bare arms. She always walked briskly, so she knew she'd be warm in a couple of minutes. Besides, she loved to feel the air on her skin. She loved all of nature. As she strode away from her back porch, beneath the tall pines, she immediately felt more at ease. It was ironic, in a way. Walking in the woods and open countryside brought back the strongest memories of her mother. The two of them had spent hours searching out-of-doors for medicinal herbs. Her mother had had a wonderful knowledge of healing plants. She'd worked as a nurse in the local hospital, and the hospital patients were often treated to herb teas that Mrs. Florence brewed for their individual conditions. The doctors at the hospital knew what her mom did and didn't seem to mind. Several of them swore her teas worked better than any medicine.

But what the doctors didn't know was that it was her mom's touch that was the real healer. Julia's gift in this area was nothing compared to her mom's. Her mom could take away a fever simply by putting her hand on someone's forehead. Yet it wasn't all that simple. There was a price to be paid. Julia knew her mom "took on" part of the sickness from those she cured. Usually it was only a small portion. Once when her mom helped a baby with a life-threatening lung infection, she immediately developed a mild cough, which lasted a couple of days. A cough was a small price to pay for a life, Julia realized, but she always worried that her mom was taking on too much. That all the small prices would one day add up to something serious.

It was that girl who killed her. The one from the motorcycle accident.

Julia's mother had died of a sudden cerebral hemorrhage. It said so on her death certificate. She died on Friday, June fourteenth, at six thirty-five in the evening. But Julia knew her mom had filled out her own death certificate a week earlier when she'd tried to heal a severely injured teenage girl. The girl had been brought to the hospital with massive head injuries. A five-hour operation by the best neurosurgeon in the county had failed to stop the buildup of innercranial pressure. Her mother had sat with the girl for three days, and when she'd finally gone home, Julia remembered, she had been white as a bedsheet and drained of all energy. She'd gone straight to bed for two days and hadn't even been awake when the hospital called to say the girl was dead. And then, two days after that, her mother had joined the girl.

It had all been for nothing, Julia thought.

It had also been a mistake. Hadn't her mother warned her against such extraordinary intervention? Why had she gone against her own advice?

"We're not gods, Julia. We're helpers. That's all. People have called us terrible things in the past. But that was only because they didn't understand us. That understanding is for the future, a time not long from now. You may live to see it. Then perhaps you can work openly, but for now, keep your gifts to yourself. Serve in what way you can, without attracting attention to yourself. Never flaunt your abilities. Never think you hold the power of life and death. Only God has that power. When it's a person's time, nothing can save them."

Yet her mom had tried to save a girl whom the doctors said had no chance. Why? Julia didn't know. She considered calling her aunt to ask her opinion, but Julia didn't really trust the woman. When her mom had died, Julia's aunt had shown no sign of grief, and Mrs. Florence was her own sister. Julia wondered if her aunt had foreseen her mom's death. Her mother had hinted that the woman could see the future.

Now there was a witch.

The last words her aunt had said to Julia three months earlier were "You watch yourself, girl." Her aunt hadn't been concerned about Julia's welfare. She was telling Julia not to abuse her powers, or else she would come after her to stop her. That was how Julia had taken the remark, at least.

Julia didn't know how old the tradition of Helpers was. Her mother said it probably went back to the beginning of mankind. The gifts followed certain bloodlines and were only passed on to females. Often the gifts didn't follow unbroken from one generation to the next. Her mother said that the gifts could disappear for centuries and resurface depending on the needs of a given time. It made Julia wonder about the needs of this time and how she would help.

The only other Helpers Julia knew were friends of her aunt's. They were a severe lot, and she and her mother had kept away from them.

"They are so busy, Julia, trying to help the world that they've forgotten how to help themselves. They've forgotten how to be happy, and it is a happy man or woman who helps the world most."

Julia took a deep breath. She could taste the approaching autumn and was glad. The change of seasons always inspired her. She would shake off her gloom, she promised herself. She promised it to her mother as well. She knew her mom was near. When Julia walked in the woods, she could feel her mother stirring inside her.

The pond she was moving toward was located a mile from her house, at the base of a granite hill that thrust so precipitously out of the earth it could have been a pillar raised by ancient gods. Julia had climbed the hill once, and only once. The sides were steep, and it had taken her the better part of a day to creep back down—and she was no coward when it came to risks. The climb had been worth it though. She had reached the top just when the sun was directly overhead. Looking straight down on the sun reflecting in the perfectly circular pond, she had found it easy to imagine that down was up, and vice versa—the reflection was that clear. For some reason the perception had filled her with extraordinary joy. For a few seconds she felt as if she could step off the granite tower and not fall. She would only be stepping into the sky, she thought. Into the sun.

Fortunately for her mortal bones, she remembered that her gifts did not include the ability to fly.

It was when she sat beside the pond and stared into the water that she saw things that were happening far off. The water had to be perfectly still, and there had to be sunlight shining on it. Julia had no idea how her gift worked. It was just there, a part of her, like her long red hair. She remembered the first time she had seen. She was ten. She had been hiking with her mother, looking for plants and flowers, and had gotten tired, so she sat down to rest beside the pond. Her mother continued to explore around the base of the granite pillar. She thought she had dozed off and was dreaming, because suddenly she could see her mother pulling roots from the ground, but she knew that her mother was not in sight. She looked up and scanned the area. Yes, she thought, it was definitely a dream. She was alone.

But it was a strange dream. She did not have to awaken from it. Plus, it took only a moment to slip back into. She gazed into the water again, and again saw her mother. Only now, her mother was hiking around the granite hill. Julia followed her the whole way, her eyes focused down into the pond. When her mom came into view—*real* view—Julia was pleased to see that she was carrying the same plants she had watched her pluck from the other side of the hill. Julia told her mom what had happened, and her mother wasn't surprised. She gave Julia only two rules concerning the gift: she wasn't allowed to spy on other people, and she couldn't look in the pond when the moonlight was shining on it.

Julia asked what was so special about the moonlight, but her mom never explained. Yet she spoke the rule so sternly that Julia never considered violating it.

Her mother called her gift "viewing."

It was fun. Whenever Julia felt the need to get away, she could sit by the pond and roam across the globe. Distance didn't seem to matter. The images were always clear. Sometimes she asked herself if she actually saw the pictures in her head and not on the surface of the water. It didn't matter. She could direct the vision at will. If she wanted to go to Africa, she was in Africa. She saw baby lions playing with one another, grown lions chasing zebras across parched plains. She visited Rome to see the pope say mass. She went to India and watched as pilgrims hiked up icy mountains to holy temples.

Not everything she viewed, however, was beautiful. Sometimes she got trapped in places she didn't want to be. *Trapped* was probably the wrong word. She could always stop the visions, but sometimes she was held by a morbid curiosity that she was unwilling to break. For example, once she found herself in a Chinese prison in which young men and women were being executed. The firing squad was lined up, and one by one the victims—they looked like college students—were trooped out and blown away. It was horrible. The students screamed for mercy, and then

9

they were lifeless corpses. Julia prayed to leave, to be back beside her pond in Idaho, but something kept her there. Later, when she asked her mother about it, her mother's answer surprised her.

"The greater the gift, the greater the responsibility. You have to learn how to use it, and you won't learn unless you see both the bad and the good—the humane and inhumane. If you find yourself stuck some place— don't resist. You are right: it was you who brought you there. It is that part of you that is separate from this world that is trying to teach you about this world."

Julia only looked into the pond once since her mother had died. She had tried to view beyond the world, into space, into the heavens. But she had run into an invisible wall and realized then that she could see no higher than the greatest birds could fly. Her viewing was bound to the world, for good or bad, and the realization filled her with profound sadness. She could see so much, but she couldn't see the one person who mattered most to her. Sometimes Julia wondered if she would ever see her mother again, even in the next world.

She reached the pond twenty minutes after talking to Amy. By then the sun had dipped so that it reached the treetops, and the light on the water was a deep orange. Julia took a seat at the eastern edge of the pond, facing west. It was a small body of water, no more than forty feet across, but deep. Once she had tried to swim to the bottom, but she had been unsuccessful. She assumed the pond was fed by an underground stream—no surface water flowed into it, and even in the heat of summer, the water level remained constant.

At present the water was as glassy as the surface of a

10

mirror. Staring at the reflection of the trees against the backdrop of the burning sunset, Julia imagined she was looking at a forest fire. Sitting there she didn't know why she had decided to go to the pond. There was nothing in particular she wanted to see. She had just acted on the spur of the moment. But maybe she had come to the pond because she had not used her gift in three months; and like an old friend, she had missed it.

I may as well see what Amy's wearing so that I don't wear the same thing.

Julia and Amy were both five-five, both slender. They often exchanged clothes. Julia no longer knew which outfits in her closet were hers and which belonged to Amy.

Julia closed her eyes and took several slow, deep breaths. The air was rich and heavy with fragrance. A small meadow lay to the south of the pond and granite hill, and it was wild with flowers. The grass beneath her bottom was thick and comfortable. Immediately she began to relax. For several seconds she imagined that she was stepping into the pond and sinking deep into its waters. The technique had come as her viewing had—unbidden. Her mind had to be as calm as the water for her to view. The feeling of sinking always brought with it a strange euphoria and dissolved her day-to-day worries. When she felt herself mentally touch the bottom of the pond, she opened her eyes and looked.

She saw Amy's kitchen. Amy and Scott were sitting at the table eating. Amy was having a small salad, and Scott was working on two huge hamburgers. Scott had never had a weight problem, but over the summer he had developed a respectable belly. The two of them were laughing, and Julia smiled to herself. But she couldn't hear what they were laughing about. It was sight, and sight alone, that operated in her visions. Her mother had once spoken about that.

"In most people there is usually one sense that is keenest. Some people need strong glasses to watch TV or read a book, but they can hear a pin drop across the room. In other people it is the reverse. Your gift is an extension of eyesight. I know that your eyes aren't that strong, but your gift is operating inside rather than outside. My gift is related to touch. You also have something of that, too, which is very unusual—to have two refined senses. The reason I can take away pain is that I can feel it when I touch it. It's that simple. When you can really feel another's burden, you can make it a part of yourself and take it away."

Julia had asked her mother where she took the pain, and she said she gave it to God. Julia liked the answer at the time. Until God took her mother away.

Julia tried to read Scott's lips. She wasn't worried about spying. She suspected Scott was talking about her, and she thought it only fair that she should know what he was saying. Sometimes she wondered how Scott felt about her. They had been friends since the age of five and they loved each other, but occasionally Amy—who was even closer to Scott—hinted that Scott loved her in a romantic way. That bothered Julia. She really did want a boyfriend, but she didn't want to lose one of her best friends to get one—and she knew it wouldn't work out. They had known each other for too long, and Scott was too crazy. Look at him right now, she thought. He took a bite of one hamburger, put it down, then took a bite of the other.

It was hard to read his lips when his mouth was full of food.

Besides, she wasn't attracted to Scott. It wasn't his fault that he wasn't handsome in a classic way. He was definitely eye-catching, however. Even across the miles that separated them, Julia found herself leaning closer to get a better look at him. His face was perfectly round and his skin tone was ruddy—slightly orangish. She and Amy had nicknamed him the Great Pumpkin. The blue in his eyes was as bright as that of a Christmas tree light. Scott was one of those people who glowed, who was always friendly, always in a great mood. Julia watched as he reached for a bag of french fries and saw Amy poke his belly and mouth the word *fat*.

Does she know? Does she feel me?

Julia found it interesting how as soon as her attention went to Amy, her friend stopped whatever she was doing and stared into space. This was not the first time Julia had viewed Amy. Although Julia never abused her gift by viewing her friend when there was the least sign that Amy needed her privacy, Julia had checked up on her a number of times throughout the years. Each time Amy had appeared to sense her presence. Whatever Amy was doing, she would suddenly stop and stare off into space. Julia would have liked to talk to Amy about it, but that would have been paramount to confessing she was a witch.

If you want me to look away, I will.

Amy suddenly smiled. She shook her head faintly. Scott put down his hamburger and asked what was wrong. Amy shook her head again. Nothing, she said. Julia also smiled. Maybe Amy was a Helper in the

13

making. It would have been nice to have a friend her age to talk to about these things.

A cry far overhead distracted Julia. It sounded like a Cooper's hawk. Without glancing up, Julia shifted her vision from Amy's kitchen to a point directly above the pond. Julia followed the hawk as it floated effortlessly on invisible air currents, flying directly toward the setting sun. The view was glorious. The evening light caressed the treetops in shades of pink and orange.

Another day. Another night.

Actually the night seemed to be coming with unnatural speed. Like a movie set on fast forward, Julia watched the sun hurry beneath the horizon. This had happened to her before. Sometimes the viewing process compacted time, so that everything was greatly speeded up. Sometimes the reverse was true. Once she had observed a bolt of lightning strike a barn in the Midwest, and it had seemed to take half an hour. Time was another quality of the process that she had no control over.

Julia still had a sense of her body. She could feel the grass beneath her bottom and the cold air on her bare arms. She could even see the water of the pond. But she'd let herself get stuck in the nighttime sky. The better part of her was half a mile above the forest. She used the sunlight to see, and now that the sun was gone, it was hard to find her way back to where she really was. There was, however, no reason to panic. This had happened to her before. All she had to do was think of falling asleep, and the eyes in her head would close and she would awake next to the water and . . .

* * *

14

Julia woke up. She thought she was awake. She felt different, strangely light, as if she had lost most of her body weight. The feeling was not unpleasant. She opened her eyes.

It was night. The pond rested flat and serene before her. The rising moon shone on the water instead of the setting sun. Julia was immediately puzzled. Had she slept away the entire night? Like the sun, the moon rose in the east. But when she had begun viewing, she was facing west. If she hadn't been unconscious all night, had she flown across the water?

Who is that?

A figure sat across from her. In the dark it was little more than a faint outline. Julia didn't feel afraid. The figure appeared to be that of a girl her own age, with long wavy hair like hers. The girl was sitting exactly the same way she was, with crossed legs and folded hands resting in her lap. Julia wondered who she could be. She tried leaning closer for a better look. Then she noticed something else.

Oh, God, it attaches the two of us together!

A luminescent silver cord stretched across the water between them. It came out of the other figure's solar plexus and—Julia couldn't be positive, but she was pretty sure—it went into her own stomach, just below her ribcage. Now that was weird, she thought. Her mom had once spoken of a silver cord, how it connected the soul to the physical body, but Julia had never witnessed anything resembling it in all her hours of viewing. Was she seeing it now because she'd left her body? Was she dead?

Is that girl sitting over there me?

Of course it was. It looked just like her. And who else would be sitting in the forest at this time of night?

Julia was pleased that she had solved the riddle. She was also happy that she had had a new experience. She thought it would be fun to explore—at a future time—this phenomenon of out-of-body travel. But she remembered her promise to meet Amy and Scott at the game. She figured she had better get back inside her body right away.

"Never look in the moonlight, Julia."

"Why not, Mom?"

"It's dangerous. Just do as I say."

Before Julia could figure out how she was supposed to get back inside her body, her vision strayed to the moonlight on the surface of the pond. In fact, her vision moved in that direction quite deliberately, in spite of the memory of her mother's warning—or maybe because of it. She had always been curious as to what she would see in the cool white light.

Now she was trapped.

The trap was similar to when she'd accidentally stumbled upon the execution of the Chinese students. She could probably have broken it with a supreme exercise of will. Yet something about the scene held her fascinated, in a sick sort of way. It was not a typical viewing. It was as if the pond had filled with gray smoke, or as if the place she had stumbled onto was cloaked in thick fog. The images were jumbled. There was a liquor store. There was a young man in a jacket. There was a girl. There was another guy. He was holding something black and hard.

It was a gun.

Was she observing a holdup? She tried to see clearer. Who were these people? The girl looked familiar. But the two guys weren't people she knew. What was it about the first guy's jacket? It meant something. It was red, completely red. *The red jacket was important,* the vision seemed to scream at her. The vision focused in tighter on it. The second guy pointed his gun at it. For a second, the red jacket was all Julia could see. Then there was a flash of fire, and the guy in the jacket was on the floor with the girl kneeling beside him. His face was covered with blood. Julia could hardly see him anymore. But now she could see the girl more clearly.

It was the same girl who was sitting across the pond from her.

It was *her.*

Julia began to shake. This couldn't be. She couldn't be in two places at once. Never in all her viewing had she ever seen herself with other people. How could she when she was sitting all alone, deep in the woods beside a pond? It didn't matter that she happened to be out of her body at the moment. She had only one body. Plus she didn't know this boy. Why did she have to watch him die?

This vision is not natural.

Julia had seen enough. Summoning her will, she forced her vision away from the moonlight on the water. She was successful, but not before she saw a close-up of the guy with the gun. He was ugly. He had cold black eyes, a thin greasy mustache, and hatred radiated from him. Yet, like Amy, he seemed to sense her watching him. His eyes stared directly at her, his hate burning deep into her heart.

Please, God, stop this.

Suddenly Julia was free of him, and she woke up with a start, her shadow cast on the surface of the pond by the moon rising at her back. She was relieved it was over, but her relief was short-lived. As she watched her reflection in the water, it changed shape to become that of an old woman. Julia recognized the woman—it was her aunt. The woman was shaking her head. She, too, seemed angry with Julia. Then the image faded, and Julia was alone.

I'm not going to do that again. I'll never do that again.

Julia stood up and hurried toward her house. She didn't know the time. She hoped the game was still on and that her friends were still waiting for her. All of a sudden she felt as if she needed her friends.

Chapter Two

SCOTT Hague was pretending he was twenty-five years old, and Amy Belle was amazed by his performance. Scott didn't have a cent to his name, but he had great clothes and plenty of style. With his blue blazer and fake gold cufflinks, a cigar in his mouth and sweet words flowing off his lips, he had the thirty-year-old brown-haired woman he'd picked up fooled. Her name was Sally Hanlon and she was really a sad case. A waitress at a nearby coffee shop, she didn't know she was spending her only night off with a kid who hadn't graduated from high school.

"What TV station are you filming this game for?" Sally asked, a wad of gum in her mouth big enough to slur her already endangered vocabulary. She had a great wig, Amy thought. It was a shame it was on lopsided.

"It's a documentary that I'm going to sell," Scott said, his Panasonic camcorder in his lap. He had turned it on a couple of times during the first half, but only to film the cheerleaders when they did their look-how-cute-our-underwear-is routine. It was presently halftime, and the hard-working girls were feeding themselves now.

"What's it about?" Sally asked.

"I haven't decided," Scott said, patting her bare knee and puffing on his cigar. Sally looked impatient.

"I feel like I'm back in high school," she growled.

"I know the feeling," Scott said wistfully.

"What do you do, dear?" Sally asked Amy.

"I go to high school," she said. Scott had asked her to act older, too, but Amy wasn't in the mood. Scott hadn't warned her ahead of time that he was bringing Sally. Amy realized he probably hadn't decided this until Julia refused to ride with them. Neither of them had much hope Julia would show.

"You mean, you go to school here?" Sally asked, astounded.

"Yeah," Amy said, enjoying herself.

"How old are you?" Sally asked.

Amy glanced at Scott. "Twenty-two," she said. "I just can't pass math."

Sally was sympathetic. "I can never keep track of my bills at the coffee shop. I think there's just too many numbers."

"Amen," Amy said, trying not to laugh. She remembered what Scott had said in the car just before they had picked Sally up.

"She's not the smartest woman in the world, but she has a deep appreciation of nature, of all natural activities. I think she may be the one, Amy. I think this is it."

Amy took the statement to mean that Scott had finally found a woman who would go to bed with him. But he couldn't have been that hot for Sally. She was nothing to look at with sober eyes. Scott said he had first met her in a bar, when he'd been drunk. Scott had no trouble getting into bars. He really did look older, even when he wasn't dressed up. He liked to think it was because he was sophisticated. Amy thought his receding hairline had a lot to do with it.

"Do we have to watch the second half?" Sally asked Scott.

"If we want to know who wins," he said.

"But Indian Pole is already losing twenty-eight to zero," Sally complained.

"They're known for their great second halves," Amy said.

"Last year they were down by thirty-five points at halftime," Scott said.

"Did they win?" Sally asked.

Scott paused. "Not exactly. But they made it look respectable."

"It was a great game," Amy agreed.

"Where are we going afterward?" Sally asked.

"Anywhere you want, babe," Scott said.

"What's the name of your boyfriend who's playing?" Sally asked Amy.

"Jim."

"Is he still in high school?" Sally asked.

"No," Amy said. "He just likes to help out. He graduated five years ago."

"He still looks like he's in high school, though," Scott said. "He's an amazing athlete."

"I wouldn't think Saddleback High could let him play," Sally said.

Scott looked disgusted. "You're right," he said. "Those cheaters."

"Is he going out with us?" Sally asked.

"It depends what time he has to be home," Amy said.

"He lives with his parents?" Sally asked.

The conversation might have gone on and on, with Sally none the wiser, if Amy hadn't decided to give Julia a call. Scott had them sitting on the top row of the bleachers. He had a zoom lens on his camcorder and didn't need to be down front for his cheerleader shots. Amy knew Scott had made them sit out of the way so that kids at school wouldn't talk to them and blow their cover. Amy was growing rather tired of Sally. She wondered how she could accidentally get rid of her. Amy stood up suddenly.

"I want to call Julia," she said.

"Who's Julia?" Sally asked.

"A friend," Scott said.

"Do you want to come with me?" Amy asked Sally. "We could go to the snack bar."

Sally was up in a shot. "I'm starving. Do they have hot dogs?"

"That's pretty much all they do have," Amy said.

"I'll come, too," Scott said, throwing Amy a look as he got to his feet. He knew what she was doing, but he wasn't mad. Scott never got mad. He had come out of the womb smiling.

The snack bar and phones were at the north end of the field, near where the players came on and left the turf. Once down from the bleachers, Amy caught sight of Jim as he was trudging back onto the field. She waved to him and he limped toward her, his red helmet in his hand. He had taken several hard hits in the first half, but he had also scored two touchdowns. Six foot two and built like a god, he was amazingly nimble on his feet. Several colleges were interested in him.

They had met at the beginning of the summer, two weeks after Julia's mom died and two weeks before Amy left for Los Angeles for the rest of the summer. Amy was helping her father clean the backyard. It was a big yard that ended in a pile of dry weeds and dead brush as tall as their house. Her dad sent her to rent a pickup to haul the junk away. Jim worked at the rental place. He gave her the only truck they had left that day, which also happened to be a wreck. It broke down before she could get a mile down the road. After she found a phone and called the rental place, they sent Jim to help her out. He said later he was impressed that she wasn't upset.

Why would she be upset? She couldn't believe her good luck. He was that good-looking. He lifted weights regularly, and his thick dark hair was a perpetual mess; it was all she could do not to run her fingers through it. There was a gentleness to him, a shyness, and when he smiled he looked all of six years old.

He never did get the truck going. She ended up having to wait until another one was returned. She hung out at the rental place for a couple of hours, talking to Jim. She did most of the talking. She was a chatty person, especially when she was nervous. When a truck finally did come in, Jim offered to help her and her dad haul the garbage away. He said he felt guilty for wasting so much of her time. She hoped the real reason he wanted to come with her was because he liked her. He seemed to. If nothing else, her dad liked him. Jim was strong. He had the thirty-foot truck loaded in an hour. He wouldn't let her dad pay him, so her mother invited him to stay for dinner. Well, actually Amy told her mother to invite him. By the time the men returned from the dump, she and her mom had a feast on the table.

He didn't kiss her the first night. She had to kiss him. She did it when he drove her back to the rental agency to pick up her car. It was just a quick peck on the cheek, but she was glad she did it. The kiss seemed to give him the courage to ask her out. Only much later did she learn that he had never had a girlfriend before. She often wondered why.

They went out four times before she left with her mom for Los Angeles—two movies and two dinners. She sent him a postcard every other day from L.A. He didn't write her once. By the time she got back she knew he didn't care. The joke was on both of them. He had thought *she* didn't care. She had sent all her postcards to the wrong address.

"How do you feel?" she asked as Jim dropped his helmet and leaned against the fence that separated them.

"Your guys keep hitting me low," he said. "Who's number eighty-six?"

"That's Randy Classick," Scott said.

"How do you know his name?" Sally asked.

Scott shrugged. "He's a big guy."

"Did he hurt your knee?" Amy asked, concerned. She wasn't a big fan of football. She thought it was barbaric, but she kept her opinion from Jim. Her boyfriend flexed his left leg.

"It only hurts when I bend it," he said.

"How old are you?" Sally suddenly asked Jim.

"He's twenty-three," Scott said quickly.

24

"Twenty-four," Amy said.

"Is that true?" Sally asked Jim, suspicious.

Jim looked puzzled. "How old are you?" he asked Sally.

"Thirty," she said.

"You're older than me," Jim said, not wanting to get involved. He turned to Scott. "Are you filming the game?"

"Oh, yeah," Scott said. "The good parts. Where do you want to go afterward?"

"Is your friend Julia here?" Jim asked Amy.

"I haven't seen her," Amy said. "I was just going to call her."

"Hey, Amy, what are you doing with that creep?" Randy Classick called from near the goalpost. He came running over. He was Indian Pole High's biggest side of beef. Amy had gone out with him once—against her better judgment—and she wouldn't be surprised if he excelled at wrestling this year. He had made it clear he found her physically stimulating. Without slapping him, she had made it clear that she wasn't there to stimulate him. He was loud and obnoxious. He was the prototype jerk-jock. Strangely enough, Julia liked him. It was Julia who had talked her into going out with him. Julia said he was deeper than he appeared. Amy still didn't know why Julia said that, and yet she knew Julia was an excellent judge of character. It was almost as if Julia could read people's minds.

"Whatever you do, don't get into a fight with him," Amy told Jim.

Jim shrugged. "As long as he doesn't give me anything to fight about."

"This guy is the enemy," Randy said when he

reached the fence. He pointed to Jim, huffing and puffing inside his helmet. "You shouldn't be associating with him, Amy."

Amy reached through the fence and squeezed Jim's hand. "This guy is my boyfriend, and I'll associate with him all I want."

Randy was disgusted. "Your boyfriend? This wimp?"

"This 'wimp' has been kicking your ass all night," Amy said.

Randy snorted. "So he got a few lucky blocks. Wait till the second half."

"Are we going to see more cheap shots?" Scott asked.

"Who are you calling cheap?" Randy demanded. "Is that you, Scott? How come you had your paper covered in chemistry? I told you before the test that I didn't have a chance to study. You always let me cheat off you."

"Are you in his chemistry class?" Sally asked Scott angrily. The truth was beginning to sink in.

Scott was nonchalant. "When I'm not working at the station," he said, "I teach a few classes here. Isn't that right, Randy?"

"Who is this woman?" Randy asked.

"My name's Sally Hanlon," she told Randy. "How old are you?"

Randy frowned. "How old are you?"

"Thirty!" Sally yelled.

"So am I," Randy said, impressed. "Is she with you, Scott?"

"I'm not sure anymore," Scott said.

"What are you doing after the game?" Randy asked Sally.

Sally hit Scott with her purse. "You lied to me!" she screamed.

"No, I didn't," Scott said, raising his arm to protect himself.

"You go to school here!" Sally shouted.

"Well, this is a college," Scott said. "Isn't that right, Randy?"

"Yes, ma'am," Randy said. "I'm going into the pros after this game. How's about you and I get together a couple of hours from now and celebrate?"

Sally didn't answer him. She hit Scott once more with her purse and stalked off. Randy shook his head as he watched her leave.

"I bet she's a firecracker, Scott," Randy said enviously.

"That she was," Scott said.

"Who was that woman?" Jim asked.

"Now you just leave her alone," Randy warned. "You've stolen enough of this town's flesh."

"You quit hitting me low," Jim said.

"I'll hit you anywhere I can," Randy said. "What do you expect me to do? We're down by twenty-eight points."

"That isn't my fault," Jim said.

Randy thought about that a minute. Then he shook his head again. "I guess it isn't. Well, just don't embarrass us. I can't stand being embarrassed." He walked off.

"Why don't you sit out the second half?" Amy suggested. "You don't need any more bruises than you already have."

"Why don't you go take a shower now so we can leave?" Scott said. "I want to swing by Julia's house."

"Oh," Amy said. "So now we're interested in Julia again."

"Who's interested in Julia?" Julia asked. She had sneaked up behind them, which she was good at. She often appeared out of nowhere. Scott turned and gave her a big hug. He worshiped her. He wasn't alone— Amy Belle thought Julia Florence was the most intriguing girl in the whole world.

Amy had known Julia since they were twelve. They had met walking in the woods. Amy had been hiking alone, carrying on an imaginary conversation with an imaginary friend. Of course, twelve is a little old to have a make-believe friend, but Amy had only made up the friend when she was ten. What was strange was that when she met Julia, she lost all interest in her imaginary friend. She felt she had found the *real* version in Julia. Julia was the imaginary friend— beautiful, sweet, soft-spoken, brilliant, and brave. When Amy tried to describe Julia to people who had never met her, she always ran into trouble. Julia sounded too incredibly perfect.

Julia's beauty was undeniable. Her fine red hair spun to her waist in careless waves. The color changed shades with the seasons. In the summer it was shiny gold, in the winter dark and grave. Yet her eyes were always bright, two green jewels that could look right into a person. When Amy first met her, it was as if Julia knew everything about her.

Julia was very brave. The previous spring, Scott, Julia, and Amy had gone for a swim in a lake near Amy's house. The day was sunny and warm, and the water looked cool and inviting. Unfortunately, Julia was the only one to test it with her hand, and her warning that it was cold went ignored. Scott climbed a huge tree hanging over the lake and dived off it—a respectable distance from the shore. The lake wasn't simply cold—the stream that fed it was nothing but melted snow from the high mountains. Scott came up quickly. Later he was to say the shock of the cold had shut his lungs off from his windpipe. He couldn't even call for help. Almost as soon as he shot to the surface he began to sink again. Julia knew what was happening in an instant, and she walked in and swam toward him.

As chance would have it, there was an old piece of rope lying on the shore near Amy. She suspected it had been used to anchor a paddle boat because it was fairly long. Amy grabbed the rope and waded into the water. Her legs immediately felt as if they had been thrust into an arctic snow. She let the water go to her waist before she stopped. Julia had reached Scott, but she appeared to be suffering the same problem—she was cramping something awful. Yet she was doing everything possible—even at her own expense—to keep Scott's head above the water. They were both coughing.

"Julia!" Amy called. "What should I do?"

"Stay there!" Julia called. "It's cold."

"I've got a rope!" Amy called back.

"Throw it to us! Pull him out!"

"I'm coming for you!" Amy cried. They were both bobbing on the surface. Julia was in front of Scott, his blue arms draped around her neck, dead weight pulling her down. Amy was afraid she would lose them both. It was so ridiculous—they had swum in the lake since they were kids.

Yet they had never jumped in so early in the spring.
"No!" Julia screamed. "Stay there. Pull him out. I can swim if I'm not holding him. Do it!"

Amy threw Julia the rope. She missed. She tried again, and this time she was on target. Julia picked up the end and shook Scott. He was barely conscious, but he seemed to understand that he had to hold on to it. Amy quickly backed out of the water, pulling on her end with all her might. Scott's grip left much to be desired, but somehow Amy managed to drag him so that his feet could touch bottom. While he staggered to the shore, Amy turned her attention back to Julia and got the shock of her life.

Julia had gone under.

The terror Amy experienced in that moment was to haunt her for months to come. The water was flat—there weren't even any ripples on it. Amy stood paralyzed for seconds that seemed to stretch to hours. Suddenly Julia broke the surface. The muscles of her arms and legs had obviously cramped into hard knots, and she was a horrible color. Amy waded out farther and threw her the rope. Julia caught it and managed to grip it. Amy pulled her in carefully. A few seconds more and it would have been too late. In fact, Julia went under again just before she reached Amy. By the time Amy had dragged her onto the shore, Julia was hardly breathing. Scott, far from recovered, started mouth-to-mouth resuscitation on her. Amy was crying when Julia opened her eyes minutes later.

"I need a hot shower," she said weakly.

Scott sat back. "Can we take one together?" he asked.

Julia smiled. "I wouldn't want to have your heart stop twice in the same day."

Scott leaned over and kissed her. "You saved my life, girl. I owe you one."

"No," Julia said, letting Scott help her up. "That's what I'm here for."

"That's what I'm here for." Julia's mom—Amy always called her Mother Florence—had said that once when Amy asked her why she worked such long hours at the hospital. Mother Florence had been a big part of Amy's life, and now that she was gone, the other parts seemed smaller. She was the one adult Amy could tell her problems to without hearing how easy she had it compared to *"when we were kids."* Mother Florence never acted superior just because she was older. She had a childlike simplicity that made everyone feel completely at ease. When Julia and Amy walked in the woods with her, Mother Florence often sang—anything from Top Forty hits to Christmas carols. She worked hard to help the sick, but she was seldom serious.

Yet Amy's admiration for Mother Florence and Julia was not shared by everyone. There was talk about the two of them. Occasionally Amy noticed that a woman in town would go out of her way not to cross Mother Florence's path on the sidewalk. Once Amy heard a lady in the drugstore say to the pharmacist that Mother Florence and her daughter were members of a cult. Amy had tried to track down the source of the rumor but came up with nothing. People knew Amy was a friend of Mother Florence and Julia and were reluctant to speak to her. Some of them seemed to be afraid of Julia's mom.

Then again, only a handful of people behaved badly to them. The vast majority viewed Mother Florence as a hard-working nurse. Often people in town went to her for "medicines" when someone in their family was ill. She never charged a penny for her teas. Five hundred people had turned up for her memorial service.

Julia was not as well liked by her peers. The qualities that drew Amy to her friend—her calm presence, penetrating intuition, cool beauty, and fearlessness—made other girls uneasy. They thought she was stuck up, which was ironic, because Julia seldom talked about herself. She just went her own way, which annoyed other kids even more. Who was she, they'd say, to think she didn't need anybody? But they didn't know her, and Amy always defended her. Julia was not the invincible fortress many people thought. She had shown that when her mom died.

Amy had been with her when the news came about her mom. It was the last day of school. They were cleaning out their lockers when the principal appeared and asked Julia to come to his office. Right away, Julia knew it was serious. She asked Amy to come with her. The principal didn't say a word until they were seated around his big oak desk. Then he said it straight— Julia's mother was dead. Julia didn't faint or start crying. She just turned and stared at the window, where the sun shone brightly on the glass. Sucking in a deep breath, she closed her eyes, then reopened them a few seconds later and stared into the glare. For several seconds she just looked at the bright sun. Then, finally, she turned to Amy. Julia was so lost right then, it broke Amy's heart.

"I can't see her, Amy," Julia said. "Why can't I see her? I could always see her before."

Julia ran from the room before Amy could comfort

her. She went to her car and drove away. Close on her tail, Amy headed straight for Julia's house, but even there she didn't catch up with her friend. Mother Florence had died at home. There were paramedics present. They told Amy that Julia had fled into the woods the moment she'd arrived, without even entering the house to say goodbye to her mother's body. Amy didn't know how she knew, but she felt certain she would find Julia at the pond. And there Julia was, bent over and sobbing at the edge of the pond, the ends of her fine red hair dipped in the cold clear water, like trails of blood. She looked up as Amy hugged her. Now there were tears.

"I can't see her," Julia kept crying. "I can't see anything."

Since that day, Julia had kept to herself. Amy tried hard to get Julia to come to L.A. with her for the summer, but Julia said there was no point in going to another place. All places were the same to her now. Amy didn't understand what she meant and wasn't sure if she wanted to. She often worried that she was going to lose her friend, that Julia would sink beneath the surface once more and never reappear.

Yet when Julia sneaked up behind them at the game, and Scott laughed and Julia smiled, it was like old times. Amy could not have been more glad to see her.

"I, for one, have no other interest," Scott said in response to Julia's question about who was interested in her. He gave her a kiss on the cheek, and Julia playfully pushed him away.

"That's not what I saw," she said.

"What did you see?" Scott asked.

"Your *date* hitting you with her purse," Julia said.

"That wasn't my date," Scott said. "That was just someone I wanted to have sex with."

"Oh." Julia nodded. "In that case, can I be your date?"

Scott caught her eye. "Sure."

"This must be Julia," Jim said.

"It certainly is," Amy said. "Jim, meet Julia Florence. Julia, this is my one and only. Look, but please don't touch." Amy laughed. "I'd like to keep this one for myself."

Jim and Julia looked at each other. Of course, there was a fence between them and they couldn't shake hands, so Amy supposed they had to look at each other real long to make up for the barrier. But Amy began to feel just a little bit uncomfortable when the *look* stretched past five seconds and neither of them had taken a breath.

Amy was not like Julia, and she knew it. She was not beautiful. She was not mysterious. Her plain blond hair didn't glisten in the sun. The light of dawn didn't shine in her ordinary blue eyes. But she did have a great figure, and she liked to think she was funny. Scott laughed at all her jokes, and he was the school's certified comedian. It was Scott who said she was incredibly sexy. Of course, it was also Scott who had been trying to get her to go skinny-dipping with him. Not that their friendship really had romantic overtones. Scott was happy that she had found Jim. The two got along fabulously, although it was beginning to look as if Jim was never going to get used to Scott's sense of humor. For example, Jim didn't see anything funny about Scott having secretly filmed Indian Pole's football coach jumping around the showers, pretending to be a heavy-metal guitarist. Scott had made several copies of the tape, which he was prepared to sell on campus.

Amy wasn't jealous of Julia. Just because a couple of her former boyfriends had fallen in love with Julia didn't mean Julia had anything to do with it. Amy didn't suffer from poor self-esteem, a problem that distanced so many of the other girls at school from Julia. Mother Florence had once told her that jealousy was the worst of all faults because it prevented a person from being who they were born to be.

"If you're always looking at someone else, trying to imitate them, how can your natural gifts ever emerge? Julia may seem deep and wise, Amy, but she doesn't always know what's right. Particularly when she gets angry. You can help her deal with her anger. Your nature is more forgiving than hers."

Amy hadn't totally understood the remark. Julia seldom got angry, or she seldom showed her anger, anyway.

"Did lightning strike or what?" joked Scott when Julia's and Jim's stare went past the ten-second mark. Jim shook himself and blushed. Julia smiled briefly, yet her face remained serious. Amy thought she had paled slightly.

"Amy's told me a lot about you," Julia said.

"She's told me a lot about you," Jim said.

"I've never talked about either of you, myself," Scott remarked. "Hey, Jim, your teammates are calling for you. We'll catch you outside the showers after the game. Maybe we can pick up a couple of six packs and get the girls drunk and take advantage of them."

Julia put her hand on Scott's arm. There was now

35

no mistaking it—Julia was definitely upset about something. "I don't want to go to a liquor store," she said.

Scott took a step back at her seriousness. "I was just kidding."

"What's wrong?" Amy asked.

Julia ignored her. She gestured to Jim. "I notice your jersey's red and white. Are those your school colors?"

Jim touched the chest of his uniform. "Yes."

"Do you have a letterman's jacket?" Julia asked.

"Yeah," Jim said.

"What color is it?" Julia asked.

"It's completely red," Jim said. "Why?"

"Don't wear it tonight," Julia said firmly.

"He has to wear it," Amy said. "It's the only jacket he brought. What's the matter, Julia?"

Julia closed her eyes and put her hand to her head. "Nothing. Nothing's wrong."

Chapter Three 🌠

THE second half of the game went like the first. Saddleback scored another fourteen points, while Indian Pole failed to get the ball in the end zone. The only difference was that Randy had stopped hitting Jim low. It wasn't as if Randy's scruples had improved—he did knock Saddleback's quarterback unconscious with a late hit. The guy had to be helped off the field. All round the game was a disappointment to everyone, except Scott, who captured excellent footage for his upcoming documentary on cheerleader bottoms.

Julia watched the second half in a daze. She had recognized Amy's boyfriend the moment she saw him as the boy who was shot in her vision. What was even more frightening was that the vision had not just shown Jim dying, it had shown him dying in *her* arms. She didn't spend a lot of time asking herself whether the vision had been accurate. It had been accurate enough to show her someone she had never met before.

What did it mean? What could it mean?

Visions seen in the moonlight show the future.

That was why her mother had forbidden her to look in the water when the moon was in the sky. Her mom had known she wasn't ready to see what destiny had in store. Who could ever be ready to see the future? Julia did not want to. She hadn't asked for it. Why hadn't her mother told her what would happen if she did look?

She knew her warning would make me want to look even more. She knew how curious I am.

It was hard to act normal in front of the others when her mind was racing. Amy was particularly tuned into her. Amy knew something was bothering her, and that it had to do with Jim. Julia wondered if Amy thought she had dated Jim before. If only she could tell her the truth!

You've known me a long time, Amy, and there's something I never told you about myself. I'm a witch. My mom was a witch, too. That's what killed her. We come from a long line of witches. No, we don't ride brooms. We're not into black magic. We use white magic. We try to help others. We look into pools of water and see things that shouldn't be and drive ourselves crazy.

Her friend would think she was crazy if she said a word about her abilities. Julia knew she'd have to deal with the situation by herself. But what was the situation? Was the future set or could it be changed? Was that the purpose of her vision—to change what was going to happen? They'd been in a liquor store when Jim was shot. But what if she never went into a liquor store with him? What if she simply never saw him again?

But he could still die. He could walk into the liquor store alone and get blown away. I don't know the rules. No one knows the rules. I can't just turn my back on what I've seen. I must stay with him.

And she had to get rid of Jim's red jacket. The jacket had been the clearest part of the vision. Perhaps that's all it needed. A change of clothes and Jim would live.

When the game was over and they were waiting outside the locker room for Jim to appear, Randy walked by. He'd showered and changed, and he had an ugly welt under his left eye. After he'd clobbered the other team's quarterback, Saddleback's front line decided on revenge. They ganged up on him on the next play. Randy was able to walk off the field, but his helmet was cracked. Julia thought he'd gotten off lightly.

"Look what they did to me," Randy complained, holding an ice bag to his eye. "Those bastards. How can you go out with one of them, Amy?"

"They're better football players," Amy said sweetly.

"Jesus," Randy said. "Their school has five times as many kids."

"They didn't play five times as many people tonight," Scott said.

"Shut up, Scott," Randy growled. "Has that woman come back?"

"No." Scott pulled a slip of paper from his pocket. "But here's her name and number. I think you'll have better luck with her. You have more in common."

Randy stuffed the paper in his pocket. "How's that?"

Scott shrugged. "She's pretty stupid."

Randy sighed and rubbed his sore head with his free hand. "That's how I like them," he said.

"Are you in pain?" Julia asked. Randy quickly took his hand away from his head.

"No," he said. "I'm all right. I'm just a big baby. How are you, Julia? You look great. Hey, I wanted to tell you that was a shame about your mom. I only talked to her a few times, but she was always nice to me. She always made me feel better about myself. She was a special woman, your mom."

Julia lowered her head. "Thank you."

"Are you doing all right alone in that house?" Randy asked.

"Yes."

"Well, if there's anything I can do, just give me a call. Any heavy lifting you need, any work in the yard, I'll come over."

Julia looked up. "You've already done enough for me."

A year earlier Julia had been roaming the local countryside in her magical pond and saw Randy carving a face on a tree deep in the woods. It was a wonderful discovery for her. She'd seen other faces carved into the trees, but she'd never known who did them. The faces were of different people—musicians, presidents, astronauts. She watched him for only a few minutes, not wishing to intrude, and was immediately taken by his skill with a knife. It was odd—Randy wasn't even enrolled in art at school. Julia admired people who created only for themselves and didn't have to be praised.

Walking deep in the woods the past month, she'd found a tree with her mother's face carved on it. The resemblance had been uncanny. She decided Randy must have obtained a photo of her mom. The carving had touched her deeply.

"What did I ever do for you?" Randy asked.

Julia smiled. "Let's talk about it later."

"Not alone, I hope," Scott said.

"Hey, you shut up," Randy told him. "Tell me more about that woman."

"She's a waitress in Kelly's Coffee Shop," Scott said.

"Oh, she can cook then." Randy nodded. "That's good. I like a stupid woman who can cook. She was pretty hot for me, huh?"

"Just don't tell her your real age," Scott advised.

Randy left to nurse his wounds. Half an hour went by. The majority of players had cleared out and the stands were long empty. It started to get cold. Scott talked about a movie he was writing that he hoped to film the next semester. It was about a possessed answering machine. He would star in it, and he wanted Julia to do the voice of the girl who kept calling. At the end of the movie the guy would find out that he was actually dead, and that the voice in his answering machine that kept interrupting his calls belonged to his guardian angel. Julia said sure, it sounded like fun.

Scott was a whiz at writing screenplays and using his camcorder. The year before he'd won a prize for a small film he did about a kid learning to ride a bike for the first time. The judges might have had second thoughts about awarding him the prize if they'd known the kids' parents threatened to sue Scott for all the bruises their son sustained during the shooting.

Scott had gone to L.A. for the summer with Amy. She told Julia that he had dragged her to a different movie every night. Julia had missed them both terribly.

Jim finally appeared. He had his red jacket on. It was as red as blood. Julia felt weak. He was so beautiful, and Amy obviously loved him. Julia couldn't help but be attracted to him herself. He was humble and warm, different from most guys his age.

I won't let him die. If I have to break his leg and put him in a hospital. I'll keep him out of every damn liquor store in the state.

But for how long could she keep him safe? Her vision had given her no time frame. Was he supposed to get shot that night? The next one? Five years from now?

"I'm sorry to keep you waiting so long," Jim said. "My knee began to swell and our trainer insisted I ice it." He gave Amy a quick hug. "I couldn't find anyone to send word out to you."

"It's no problem," Amy said, concerned. "Is the knee OK?"

"Sure," Jim said. "It's nothing. So, what do you guys want to do now?"

"Let's go to my house," Julia said quickly.

"What are we going to do there?" Scott asked.

"Anything we want," Julia said. "No one's there. We could rent a movie."

Scott was interested. "Did you get a VCR?"

"We can rent a VCR," Julia said.

"I'm thirsty," Jim said. "Could we go somewhere for a drink?"

"I'd still like a beer," Scott said, eyeing Julia. "If that's all right with you, Julia?"

"If we can go to a bar, yeah," Julia said. "Otherwise, I don't think we should drink."

"That makes sense," Scott said sarcastically. "We can't go to a bar. I'm the only one with a fake I.D. What have you got against liquor stores?"

Julia giggled nervously. "I just don't want to walk in on a holdup."

"We could go for a drive," Amy suggested.

"Where to?" Scott asked.

"I don't know," Amy said in her most helpful manner.

"Great," Scott said. "We'll do that. We'll drive and drive, and if we don't run out of gas maybe we'll end up somewhere interesting."

Amy had come with Scott. Jim had come by himself —he'd had to be at the game early. Julia had, of course, also come by herself. They decided to take Scott's car. It was the only one with more than a quarter of a tank of gas. Scott had been serious. He meant to drive until they figured out what they wanted to do. A movie was out. It was already after eleven. Soon all the liquor stores would close. Julia figured she should be able to keep them out of a holdup. She relaxed a bit.

The boys sat in the front, the girls in back. Scott drove. The arrangement was Amy's idea. She said she wanted to talk to Julia.

"What did you mean when you said Randy had already done enough for you?" Amy asked Julia as they headed out of Indian Pole, which took all of two minutes. Scott was going south.

"He once did a favor for my mother," Julia said. "I probably shouldn't talk about it without his permission."

"Are we talking about the same hunk of meat?" Scott asked from the front seat. Julia was sitting behind Jim. She liked his hair—it wasn't cut short like that of most football players. It hung uncombed over his collar, and she had to stop herself from reaching for the brush in her purse.

"Randy's not so bad," Julia said.

"Ha," Jim said. "He didn't spend half the night rearranging your skeleton."

"You poor dear," Amy said. "Is your knee still hurting?"

Jim turned stiffly. "Now it's my neck. I must have strained it without knowing it. God, I'm going to be sore tomorrow."

"Do you have to work?" Amy asked.

"Starting at eight," Jim said. "Saturday and Sunday are their busy days. Everybody rents trucks on weekends. It's like football—a national pastime."

"You should have Julia rub your neck," Amy suggested. "She's got incredible hands."

"Nah," Jim said. "I'm all right."

"Never turn down a Julia Florence massage," Scott advised Jim. "It may be the high point of your life. I remember the time she gave me a full-body massage with baby oil on a snow-white beach in Tahiti. Remember that, Julia? It was so hot we were both completely naked."

"I don't remember every dream you have," Julia said with a laugh.

"I remember," Scott said.

"Could you rub Jim's neck?" Amy asked her.

"Amy," Jim said, "don't bother her. You can rub it."

"I'm sitting on the wrong side," Amy said. "Besides, she really is good. She's studied acupressure and polarity and stuff like that."

WITCH

"There is a pulled muscle in your neck," Julia said quietly.

Jim tried to turn and look at her. "How do you know?"

"Your neck looks like it's stuck in a vice when you turn it." Julia gave him the obvious answer, but it was not the real one. She knew because she knew. She was not her mother, but she could feel where pain radiated from in other people.

"Do you really want to rub it?" Jim asked.

Julia shrugged. "I don't mind." She glanced at her best friend. "As long as Amy doesn't mind."

"Why should I mind?" Amy said. "I know you can help him."

"You'll have to take off your jacket," Julia told Jim.

Scott nodded knowingly. "Wait till she works down to your lower back, Jim. You'll have to take off your clothes. That's what happened in Tahiti. Pretty soon you'll be helpless. But there are worse ways to go, I suppose."

Jim hesitated a second before removing his red letterman's jacket. The interior of the car was warm. Julia had him pass the jacket back to her, where she could "keep it out of his way." She was happy to have it off him. She rubbed her palms together briefly and then touched the base of his neck with the tips of her fingers. She knew very little about acupressure. She told Amy and Scott that she had studied massage techniques because the few times she had rubbed their backs and necks they had been amazed at how relaxed they felt. It was only the power of her touch that made her such an effective masseuse.

As Julia placed her hands on Jim's neck, she felt a faint current flow through her fingers. It was as if her

45

hands were opposite poles of two magnets, and Jim's flesh was a conduit that linked the poles together. Jim took a deep breath and sighed. The muscles of his neck quivered and began to relax. She hadn't even begun to massage him.

"Wow!" Jim said.

"I told you she was good," Amy said softly, watching closely.

Julia began gently to knead his muscles. It was something to do, but it wasn't necessary. The stiffness flowed from his neck like water from an overturned jar. All at once, Julia felt a wave of dizziness, and she remembered something her mother had said.

"Healing never involves ego. If you try to help someone for personal gain, even to hear grateful words of thanks, then you may or may not receive that in return. But you will surely take on their pain, and have trouble getting rid of it. It can show up in different ways. If they have a headache, you may get a stomachache. A healer is only a channel for God's love. A healer never draws attention to him- or herself. A healer is compassionate, yet unattached. This is hard to learn—unattachment in the face of pain. But if it is not learned, the healer does not last."

Her mother had not lasted.

"That feels so good," Jim said.

Julia paused to question her motives. The others had talked her into rubbing Jim's neck. She had not brought it up. Yet she had allowed herself to be talked into it because she knew that as soon as she touched him he would begin to feel better. Plus she had wanted to touch him.

How can I be unattached when he's so cute?

She reminded herself that Jim was Amy's boy-friend.

"Are you getting tired?" Jim asked.

"No," Julia said. Her dizziness subsided and she resumed massaging. She began to get a headache. It started in her temples and swiftly spread to the top of her head. It was not acute, but it made her vision blur. She knew what the problem was. She was trying to impress Jim with her massage. Her ego was totally involved.

"Isn't she amazing?" Amy asked.

"Incredible," Jim agreed, his eyes closed. "I feel like I'm floating."

"Are you still thirsty?" Scott asked. "There's a gas station up ahead. There's a small store attached."

"A Coke would be great," Jim said.

"Is that OK with you girls?" Scott asked.

"I'd like a Coke," Amy said.

"Fine with me," Julia muttered, closing her own eyes. She wrapped her hands all the way around Jim's neck, and the pain in her head increased. Still, it wasn't overwhelming. She could always have Scott get her some aspirin. As long as it wasn't a liquor store he was stopping at, she didn't care.

Julia changed her mind a minute later.

"Why don't I run in and get the stuff?" Jim suggested as they pulled up. "You keep the car running."

"Fine with me," Scott said. "Need a few dollars?"

Jim waved his hand. "I'm fine." He gave a short laugh. "If I can stand up, that is. You've got some touch there, Julia."

"Thank you." She took her hands off his neck and glanced over at the inside of the food area attached to the station. She felt groggy, and her vision still hadn't cleared. It took her several seconds to see the rows of liquor bottles lined up on the shelves.

"Could you hand me my jacket, Julia?" Jim asked.

"No," she said.

"Julia, it's cold," Amy said. "Give him his jacket."

"No," Julia said again, getting anxious. She shook her head, trying to clear her brain. What exactly had she seen in the vision? Had it been a regular liquor store? "I don't like this place. Let's go somewhere else."

"What's wrong with it?" Scott asked. "Look, I'm not going to buy beer. We just want something to drink."

"I don't need my jacket," Jim said, opening his door. Julia grabbed his arm.

"No," she said. "I'll go in. You shouldn't jump up after a massage." Julia opened her door. "I have money."

Julia didn't realize how bad her headache was until she stood. The blood in her brain seemed to drop down into her chest, and a black hand passed over her eyes. She had to grab the side of the car to keep from falling. She sat back down on the edge of the backseat.

"God," she whispered.

"What's wrong?" Amy asked.

"Headache," Julia mumbled, lowering her head to her knees, her feet resting on the asphalt outside. Cold air enveloped her, and she drew in a deep breath.

"Is it bad?" Scott asked, worried.

"No," Julia lied.

"I'll get you a bottle of Tylenol," Scott said, opening his door. "Everybody stay here. Julia, you don't sound good. We'll just go straight home when I get back."

Julia felt Amy put a hand on her back. She continued to draw in long, deep breaths. The headache decreased, but slowly. She understood that Scott had gone for the drinks, not Jim, and this reassured her somewhat. But as her strength returned, so did her anxiety. She opened her eyes to look inside the gas station. Nobody was inside—not even a man or woman at the register. Yet the place was open. She stood up again.

"I'll be back in a second," she said.

"Julia," Amy called.

"Stay here," Julia said, quickly rounding the front of the car. Scott had already picked up his goods. He was standing at the cash register, poking his head around and looking for someone to ring him up.

"Scott!" she called.

He didn't notice her. He was too busy looking the other way.

Looking . . .

God, no!

Scott finally saw someone, but not the someone he wanted. Leaning over the counter, he suddenly jerked back, dropping his six pack of Coke and bottle of Tylenol. He staggered back from the counter on unsteady legs. Julia broke into a full sprint. She crashed through the twin glass doors just as the thin mustached figure in the black leather jacket appeared. He came from the rear of the store, with a partner at his back.

It was the guy in her vision.

In his hand was a gun.

It was raised in Scott's direction.

"Stop!" Julia screamed.

Julia jumped as she had never jumped in her life.

She leapt directly at Scott's waist. Trying to outrace the bullet, or even the finger on the trigger—either would have been fine—but she had fifteen feet to cover, and no human could beat a bullet in a race, and the skinny guy's trigger finger had only a fraction of an inch to cover in the same time. She was in midair when she saw the burst of fire and heard the crack of thunder. The bullet struck Scott on the left side of the head. Red fluid spurted into the air. Julia slammed into Scott, and the two of them hit the floor.

They will die. I will make them die.

Julia's thoughts did not immediately turn to Scott. He had been shot at close range, in the head. She figured he was dead. Nor did she think about the possibility that she was about to be shot. She had a feeling—it was overwhelming in its intensity—that she could not be hurt. That nothing could hurt her. That she could not be stopped from what she had set her will to do. The feeling came to her out of nowhere, like a vision seen in a dark pond upon which no light had ever shone.

Julia jumped up from Scott. The guy in the leather jacket was retreating toward the rear of the store. He had his back to her, but the kid with him was staring directly at Julia. He was short and flabby, young and innocent, and he was holding a shotgun. Julia couldn't be sure if he was moving his shotgun from one hand to the other or if he was in the process of raising it in her direction. He didn't seem to know how to handle the weapon. Julia did not wait to see if he could. She struck with her mind.

What happened in that moment was never clear to Julia. It seemed as if her two abilities—to see far off and to heal by touch—merged and twisted into something alien. In her mind the short fat guy had moved toward her within touching distance. She reached for him with the intent of ripping his heart from his chest. Her vision blurred again. This time a red hand passed over her eyes.

The short guy lost his grip on his shotgun. He slumped back against the wall, his face white. The skinny guy caught him as he fell and glanced over his shoulder at Julia. Their eyes met, and the guy flashed a grin that was more of a sneer. It was almost as if he knew about her vision and was telling her that, despite everything she had seen, she couldn't stop him. He raised his gun and pointed it at her face.

Julia ducked to the floor as a shot sounded.

The box of cereal at her back exploded.

You are not invincible. His bullets will kill you!

Julia immediately rolled into the only other aisle, away from Scott, putting a row of bakery products between her and the counter. Shifting into a crouching position, she peered over a rack of bread.

The two guys were gone.

"Amy! Jim!" Julia yelled. She ran to the counter, catching a glimpse of the hoods as they went out the back door. The guy with the mustache was still helping his partner. The fat guy couldn't have been too hurt, though, because a moment later Julia heard two motorcycles roar to life. Amy and Jim pounded through the front door just then.

"Oh, Jesus!" Amy cried, dropping to her knees beside Scott. The floor must have been dirty. The puddle of blood around Scott's head was almost black. The dirty liquid soaked into the knees of Amy's white pants. Out back, the engines of the motorcycles revved. Julia grabbed Jim's arm.

"We have to go after them," she said.

"Who?" Jim asked, his eyes on Scott.

"The guys on the bikes!" Julia said, pointing toward the rear of the store. "They're getting away."

"No," Jim said. "We're staying here."

"No!" Julia yelled. "I'm going to kill those guys."

"Julia," Amy pleaded, Scott's head in her hands, tears pouring over her cheeks. "We have to take care of Scott."

Julia shook her head bitterly. "He's dead."

Jim knelt beside Scott and felt his neck for a pulse. Then he leaned over and put his ear to Scott's chest.

"He's still breathing," Jim said. "There's a chance." He put his hand on the head wound, trying to stop the bleeding. His fingers were immediately soaked red. He nodded to the phone behind the counter. "Dial nine-one-one, Julia. Get an ambulance here immediately."

"He's got to be dead," Julia said miserably, staring at her childhood friend with blank eyes and shaking her head. The noise of the motorcycles soared higher before diminishing. The hoods were fleeing on the road Scott had just driven, back in the direction of Indian Pole.

"He's alive!" Jim snapped. "Amy, call. Be quick."

Julia closed her eyes. She heard Amy dialing behind her. She heard the sound of the motorcycles growing fainter. She didn't see anything, however. The sun wasn't out—the clear water wasn't in front of her. She opened her eyes. The puddle of blood had grown, and now it was staining the soles of her shoes. She stepped over to Scott and plopped down onto the floor next to him, with Jim across from her. Jim was continuing to press against the hole in Scott's head. Julia told him to stop. Jim shook his head.

"I've got to stop the bleeding," he said.

"Only I can stop it," Julia said.

Scott, what about the beach? What about the white sand? I loved all your dreams. I love you.

"Julia," Jim began.

"No," Amy said suddenly and knelt beside Scott's feet. She motioned for Jim to move aside. "Let her try."

Jim frowned. "What?"

"Let her try," Amy repeated. Then in a softer voice: "Can you do it, Julia?"

"I can do anything," Julia whispered. She reached out and took Scott's head, his blood warm and sticky beneath her shaking fingers. It was true he was still alive, but she knew life could run to the end of a fine thread before it snapped and was gone. Her mother had told her that. Her mother had told her a lot of things, except how to ask God to remove a bullet from the brain of your friend. Julia didn't even bother to ask God for help. She held Scott and closed her eyes and let the pain pour into her.

She saw and felt horrible things.

There was a black wave on the horizon, a tidal wave that reached high into a black sky. There were no stars, no sun or moon. The air was filled with the poisonous vapors of her vision. Julia tried to hold her breath, to concentrate on what she had to do to bring Scott back. But the vapors entered her lungs, and she began to cough. The wheeze in her chest hissed in her ears like the sound of approaching death.

My death, Scott. Neither of us was supposed to come this way.

Julia let out a cry of terror. She released Scott's head and collapsed in Amy's arms, sobbing uncontrollably.

"I can't do it," she moaned. "I'll die if I do it."

"I understand," Amy said, stroking her hair.

Chapter Four

Scott had been on the operating table for three hours, and they still weren't done. Amy wondered if she would ever see him alive again. They would wheel him out with a sheet draped over his face, she kept thinking, the blood soaking through the material. They would tell her with sad faces that they had done everything they could. Then she would faint, and they would catch her. They would wake her up, then give her something to help her sleep. But she wouldn't sleep. She would stare at the ceiling all night and try to imagine a world without Scott.

After calling the ambulance, Amy had found the owner of the gas station tied up in the back, unconscious. He had been struck hard on the back of the head, but the doctors said he would be fine.

At present a detective was questioning the three of them. They sat in a cramped waiting room, across the hall from a larger room where Scott's family had assembled. Amy had spoken to Scott's mother for a few minutes, and it was the hardest thing she had ever done. The woman had no hope.

"Where did he get shot, Amy?"

"In the head."

"The bullet went in my son's head?"

"Yes, Mrs. Hague. I'm so sorry."

"He's finished."

Amy told her they couldn't think that way, but Scott's mother just shook her head. She refused to go to the hospital chapel to pray with Amy. Amy had prayed—she believed in miracles.

She also believed that Julia had known what was going to happen.

"Let me get this straight," Lieutenant Crawley said. "Scott went into the gas station first, but Julia ran in after him a minute later."

"That's correct," Julia said, her voice flat, her expression empty.

"Why?" Crawley asked.

Julia shrugged. "I don't know."

"Can't you do any better than that?" Crawley asked.

"Nope," Julia said.

"Did you see anything that made you suspect a robbery was in progress?" Crawley asked.

"Nope," Julia said.

"You're not being very cooperative, young lady," Crawley said.

"I guess not," Julia said, staring straight ahead.

"Lieutenant," Amy interrupted, "we told you what happened. Julia's told you twice. Why do you keep asking her the same questions?"

Lieutenant Crawley didn't appreciate the interruption. He was a funny guy. When he had first showed up at the hospital, Amy thought he was very professional, very thorough. But then he went over the exact same questions for a second and third time. Amy decided he might be confused after being awakened in the middle of the night. But he didn't look confused. On the contrary, he was sharply dressed, with a black sports coat and tailored gray slacks. Although he must have been close to forty and was almost bald, he was handsome in a no-nonsense sort of way. He had crushed Amy's hand when he shook it. Amy suspected he had served as a marine.

"I'm repeating myself because I'm not satisfied with your answers," Crawley said. "I understand Scott is your friend and how much you must be hurting, but the best way to catch the kids who shot him is to tell me everything you know."

"What do you want to know that I haven't told you?" Julia asked.

"Why did you run into the store after Scott?" Crawley asked.

"I had a feeling something was wrong."

"What gave you this feeling?" Crawley asked.

"I didn't see anybody behind the cash register," Julia answered.

"And that made you panic?" Crawley asked.

"I didn't panic."

"But Jim here says you rushed into the gas station like you knew something was wrong," Crawley said.

"I just had a feeling," Julia said. "What can I say?"

"When did you get this feeling?" Crawley asked.

"I don't know. When we got to the gas station."

"But Jim said that you were worried about stopping for a drink the whole night," Crawley said.

"I don't think people should drink and drive," Julia said.

"Lieutenant," Jim said, "all I said was that Julia seemed to be on edge the whole night. I wasn't implying that she—"

"I know what you meant," Crawley interrupted. He studied the notepad in his hand. "When you entered the store, Julia, you said you saw two guys, one with a handgun and the other with a shotgun. The skinny one pointed his gun at Scott, and you tried to knock Scott out of the way. But before you could reach him, Scott got shot in the head."

"That's correct," Julia said.

"Then you jumped up, and the fat kid pointed his shotgun at you."

"He didn't exactly point it at me," Julia said.

"What exactly did he do?"

"He shifted it in his hands."

"And then?"

"Then he stumbled against the wall," Julia said. "His partner caught him. Then his partner shot at me."

"But you dodged the shot?" Crawley asked.

"Yes."

"You jumped out of the path of the bullet?"

Julia shrugged again. "I guess so."

"You must be pretty quick."

Julia stared at him. "May I ask you a question, Lieutenant?"

"Yes."

"Do you think I knew those two guys?"

"Did you?" Crawley asked.

"No," Julia said. "I told you I didn't. Why do you think I'm connected to this robbery?"

Crawley was insulted. "I never said—"

"Not in so many words," Julia said, continuing to stare at him. "Let's not play games. I know who *you* are. I remember you."

Crawley raised an eyebrow. But he didn't give a damn. "Then you remember that I ask a lot of questions."

"What are you two talking about?" Amy asked.

"It's nothing," Julia said. "Isn't that right, Lieutenant?"

"Yeah, it's nothing." Crawley stood. "I'm not through with any of you."

"That makes us feel a lot safer," Julia said sarcastically.

Crawley sucked in his gut and let out his air in a short burst. He turned his attention down the hall in the direction of the operating theaters. "I hope your friend lives," he said simply as if to make amends.

"Thanks," Amy said. When the detective was gone, she turned to Julia. "What was that all about?"

Julia leaned her head against the wall. "Jim, could you get me a Coke from the machine? I'm dying for a drink."

Jim jumped up. "Sure."

"Jim?" Amy said.

"Yeah?"

"Could I have one, too?"

"OK."

When Jim was gone, Julia glanced at her friend out of the corner of her eye. Amy hadn't gotten over seeing the venom that burned in Julia's eyes after the shooting. Julia had wanted an eye for an eye. Amy felt a chill. Julia had wept at the gas station after touching

Scott's head, but now her tears were dried up and she seemed to be thinking of revenge again.

Why does that scare me? Because she's capable of getting it?

Had Julia known those guys? Amy had doubts of her own.

"I met Lieutenant Crawley a year ago," Julia said. "You remember that paper warehouse that burned down outside of town? I was in the area when it happened. It was a Saturday—there was no one there. I saw the smoke and ran to the nearest house for help. Crawley was there, but he wouldn't do anything."

"Why not?"

"Because it wasn't his house—I found out later it was his mistress's. Crawley tried to act like he wasn't even a cop when I saw him at the door. But I knew who he was. I'd seen him around. He made me go somewhere else to call the fire department. By then the warehouse was an inferno. I told the police afterward that Crawley wouldn't let me use his phone. He got into trouble."

"I don't understand," Amy said. "Why didn't he just call the fire department?"

"I think he panicked. He was in the wrong place at the wrong time. He was afraid of being found out. He tried to shoo me away. For all I know, his wife left him."

"How could she have found out?"

Julia chuckled bitterly. "She wouldn't have found out if Crawley had accepted his superiors' reprimand and kept his mouth shut. But he tried to convince them that I was lying, that I hadn't talked to him that day. He tried to discredit me. He brought up evidence that I must have started the fire."

"You're kidding!"

"I'm not. He said there was no way I could have seen the smoke when no one else had—unless I started the fire."

"How did you see it?" Amy asked.

Julia paused. "What do you mean?"

"What were you doing out there?"

"I was just driving around."

"How did you know Crawley was a cop?"

"I told you, I'd seen him around."

"But isn't he a plainclothesman?"

Julia spoke carefully. "I didn't say I went to his mistress's house because I knew a cop was there. The place was near the warehouse. He just happened to be there."

"I understand," Amy said, surprised by Julia's serious tone. Julia's story about the fire disturbed Amy, and she wasn't sure why.

I just don't want to walk in on a holdup.

Amy knew, of course, that what she was thinking was impossible.

Julia saw smoke tonight—before the guns were fired.

"What's wrong?" Julia asked.

"Nothing. Everything." Amy shook her head and dabbed at her eyes. She'd already gone through a box of tissues since they left the gas station. The waiting and not knowing was killing her. Would the doctors never come out? "You think Crawley's trying to implicate you in this holdup so he can show you could have been involved in the warehouse burning down?"

Julia sighed. "I think Crawley's an idiot who doesn't know what he's doing."

Jim returned with the Cokes, but they never opened them because the surgeon appeared just then. He was a short man with incredibly hairy arms. He hadn't changed out of his green operating gown, and there were specks of blood on it still. He looked exhausted. He asked Scott's parents if they wanted everyone to hear the news, and they nodded their heads.

The news was not good.

"The bullet entered the left side of Scott's skull here," the doctor said, tapping his own head. "Had it continued on a straight course, it would have caused severe damage to the frontal lobes of his brain. But what it did—and this is not uncommon among head-shot victims—was snake around the perimeter of the skull and lodge back here." The surgeon touched the back of his head on the left side. "Fortunately, the bullet remained intact, and we were able to remove it whole."

"Then he'll be OK?" Scott's father asked. Amy had grown up only a block away from Scott. Mr. Hague had always been there, pitching them baseballs, taking them to the movies, buying them ice cream. Like Scott, he was always filled with ready laughter. Tonight, though, he looked as if he might never laugh again. No one had loved a son more.

The doctor shook his head. "Scott has suffered a serious head wound," he said. "There is extensive bleeding and tissue damage. The fine membrane that filters what enters the brain—it is often called the brain barrier—has been badly torn. Infection is a major problem. The problem of swelling is worse and more immediate. Because the brain sits in a tight space, it has no room to expand. Swelling causes pressure, and brain cells die when subjected to pressure. We have left Scott's skull open a bit, with a tube draining to the outside. But Scott is running a high fever, which is one sign that the swelling is building."

"Is he going to die?" Mrs. Hague asked.

The doctor shook his head. "I don't know."

"Is he going to die?" the woman insisted. The doctor looked long into her face. He started to say something, then changed his mind. He said what he thought.

"I'm sorry. Scott probably won't last the night."

Amy heard the words. She had been waiting to hear the words. And now that they had been spoken, she didn't have to wait any more. The prognosis stabbed at something inside her, killing it, putting it out of its misery. She felt suddenly cut off from her surroundings, from her body even. She drifted in a gray void. The doctor continued to talk, but she couldn't understand what he was saying. Time took on a strange quality—moving both fast and slow at the same time. Finally the doctor turned and walked away. Jim put a hand on her shoulder and shook her gently, bringing her out of her stupor.

"Do you want to see him?" Jim asked.

"What?" she mumbled.

"The doctor said we could see him," Jim said.

Amy felt confused. Close family should be the only ones allowed in to see a patient after a serious operation. Then she realized the truth: the doctor didn't think it would make any difference.

He's letting us say goodbye.

"Yes," Amy said. Let's go."

They didn't get in immediately. Scott's family was in front of them, and Julia wanted to wait until they were gone. Amy caught herself staring at Julia. At the gas station, Amy had had reason for wanting Julia to touch Scott's head. For a long time she had known of the wonderful magic in Mother Florence's hands. Mother Florence had not hidden it from her. A couple of years earlier, when Amy had been suffering from a migraine—she used to get them at least once a month—Mother Florence put her hands on the back of her head and the pain vanished in a matter of seconds. In fact, the headaches never returned. When Amy asked what she had done, Mother Florence said it was a gift and that it couldn't be explained.

"But keep it private. Don't even tell Julia what I did. It isn't me who does it, anyway. It's God."

Amy asked if Julia had the same gift. Mother Florence said yes. Amy wasn't surprised. The few times Julia had trimmed her hair, Amy loved the feel of Julia's hands on her head. They radiated warmth and love.

Amy had known Julia could get rid of Jim's sore neck.

But what Julia felt when she touched Scott terrified her. Why? Amy wanted to know.

Finally they were able to see Scott. His cubicle in intensive care was separated from the other cubicles by drawn curtains. The air smelled strongly of blood and medicine. Amy wondered if she should have stayed outside. She had a weak stomach. The bandages around Scott's head were already soaked red. A thin white sheet covered him, and there were so many tubes and needles going into his body that she cringed at how tenuous his hold on life must be. A pump hissed up and down beside his head. He was being artificially ventilated.

He can't even breathe for himself.

His color also shocked her. He had none. He was bone-white.

"This should never have happened," Jim said sadly. "It should have been me who went in that store."

"Don't say that," Amy said, unable to pry her eyes away from Scott, even though he no longer looked like Scott or anyone she had ever known. The left side of his face was a swollen mass of purple. His lips were cracked and bleeding.

"It's true," Jim said, still speaking. He had turned to Julia. "You saved my life when you stopped me."

"I didn't save anybody's life," Julia whispered. Amy tore her eyes from Scott to look at Julia, who was clearly dazed. Yet the hardness around her eyes and mouth remained. She held her clenched hands near her heart. It was as if a part of her wanted to touch Scott, while another part was telling her to beware.

"What do you think?" Amy asked her.

"I don't," Julia said.

"Is he going to die?" Amy insisted.

"I'm not a doctor," Julia said. She added, "His light is very weak."

"Huh?" Jim asked.

"Is there anything you can do?" Amy asked.

Julia looked up. "What would you have me do, Amy?"

Amy held her eye. "Whatever you can."

Julia drew in a short breath. She barely nodded. "You know?"

"Yes," Amy said.

"Who told you? My mother?"

"Yes."

Julia turned her attention back to Scott. "I'm not my mother."

"I don't understand what you two are talking about," Jim said.

Julia's gaze shifted to Jim. The dark light glittered deep inside her green eyes. "How would you like to catch the guys who did this to Scott?" she asked.

Jim was interested. "How? Do you know who they are?"

"In a way," Julia said. "I can find them."

"You should tell the police what you know," Amy said.

"The police!" Julia snorted. She gestured to Scott. "Do you think any of them give a damn about what's happened here?"

"If you can find them, I'll make them pay," Jim said. "You can bet on it."

Julia smiled thinly. "That's just what I wanted to hear." She turned to leave. "Let's go. Stay here, Amy."

Amy jumped after Julia, grabbing her by the arm. "What are you going to do?" she demanded.

Julia paused, regarding her without emotion. "What I have to do."

Amy felt another chill. She didn't know exactly what Julia had in mind, but she felt intuitively that it was wrong. "What would your mother say?" she asked.

"I don't know. I can't ask her, can I?"

"Forget those guys," Amy said. "What's done is done. Your place is here with Scott. You can help him."

Julia glanced over at Scott. For a moment the anger in her eyes vanished. Her lower lip trembled, and a teardrop glistened below her right eye. "I can't ask Scott now, either," she said softly.

"Stay," Amy begged. "Please?"

Julia hugged her. But when she let go, she was shaking her head. "I can't," she said. "I have to set things right."

"By killing somebody?"

"We'll see," Julia said. "Goodbye, old friend."

"Goodbye," Amy said sadly, not knowing if the "old friend" was meant for her or Scott.

Jim left with Julia. He barely nodded a quick goodbye to Amy.

He wants her as much as he wants revenge.

Amy turned back to Scott and picked up his cold hand. She kissed it and tried to warm it in her own hands. She was afraid she'd never see Julia or Jim again.

"I'll stay with you," she told Scott. "You're all I have left."

Chapter Five

THEY drove to Julia's house. It was near dawn. The air was cold and silent. They still had Scott's car. Julia told Jim to hide it in the back.

"Why?" he asked.

"I don't want anyone to know we're here," she said.

"Are you worried about Lieutenant Crawley?"

"No."

My aunt saw what I saw. She saw me. Did she see what happened?

Julia didn't consider turning to her aunt or her aunt's friends for help. She knew her aunt would never forgive any abuse of power. The aunt would remind her that she had been warned never to use the moonlight, and she would probably try to punish her.

Who really knows what that old hag could do?

But Julia wasn't afraid. She knew she could defend herself now—now that she had taken care of that fat kid. She had never realized how powerful she was. She would take care of the other one just as easily. She didn't need the old woman's help.

Jim drove the car into the pine trees behind her house. After they parked, she walked him to her back door and gave him her keys. "I'll be back in an hour or two," she said.

"Where are you going?"

"To check with somebody I know who lives deep in the woods. She'll know who these guys were. Don't ask me how—just trust me on this. I have to go alone because she guards her privacy."

Jim studied Julia's old brick house. It had been built before the First World War. Ivy and bushes all but obliterated the walls, so that it looked like a house from the Middle Ages, when people believed in witches.

"I can see she's not the only one who guards her privacy," Jim said.

"I haven't always lived alone," Julia said.

Jim nodded. "Amy told me about your mom. It must have been hard for you."

"I get by."

"What about your dad?"

"I don't have one."

"You must have had one some time or the other."

Julia looked into the woods. With the faint eastern light behind them, the trees appeared strangely watchful. She wasn't afraid of her aunt or her aunt's friends, but she couldn't free herself from the feeling that someone was on her tail.

"My father left when I was very young—an infant," she said quietly. "When my mother died, the state said I had to have a guardian. My aunt was put in charge of me, and she's demanded that I move in with her. But I've stalled them both, and I'll be eighteen in a few months. Then they can't touch me."

"It must get lonely living outside of town with no one around."

"I'm used to it," she said. Jim had his hands stuffed in his pockets and his shoulders hunched. He was shivering, but the cold didn't affect her in the slightest. She was glad he had come with her—he was strong and no coward. She didn't know what was going to happen, but she had a feeling it could get nasty before it was over. She was confident she'd be able to locate the hoods in the pond.

What about my vision? Did Scott take the bullet meant for Jim? Is the vision done with? It must be.

Still, she knew she'd have to keep an eye on Jim.

"Get inside before you catch pneumonia," Julia said. "If anyone comes to the door, don't answer."

"All right." He stared at her for a moment. "Can I ask you something, Julia?"

"Sure."

"Have we met before?"

"Not that I know of. Why?"

"You look so familiar. When you were introduced to me at the game, you probably noticed that I kept staring at you."

She blushed. "I thought you were entranced by my beauty."

He smiled. "That must have been it." He lowered his head. "You are very beautiful."

"So is Amy."

He looked up quickly. "I'm sorry. That's not what I meant. I wasn't trying to—you know. I'm happy with Amy."

"I know you are. She's a great girl." She added, "I'm the one who should be sorry."

He didn't catch her meaning. "Why should you be sorry?"

"Because I'm a liar," she said thoughtfully. It was finally hitting home.

He's not supposed to be here. He died in my vision. He's like an angel, still walking the earth.

"What did you lie about?" Jim asked.

"We have met before."

"Where? When?"

"In heaven," she muttered. Then she shook herself. "Never mind me. Go inside and rest. Eat what you want. I'll be back soon." She reached out and hugged him. He was good to hold. He hugged her in return, and she could hear the beating of his heart through his red jacket. "You're beautiful, too," she said.

"You think so?"

She let go of him and smiled. But she had to force the smile—because suddenly she did feel all alone. He didn't belong to her. No one did. And Scott was dying.

"I do," she said.

Julia walked briskly, without fatigue. She reached the granite hill and the pond in less than fifteen minutes. The walk did little to settle her mind, which continued to race with thoughts of what she'd do to the guy who had shot Scott. She began to wonder if she'd be able to use the fist in her mind a second time. Her mom once said that some gifts came only once. Then again, Julia doubted that her mother would have called her mental punch to the fat kid's guts a gift.

"What would your mother say?"

That was a good question. Julia knew what her mother's answer would have been. Her mother had abhorred the idea of revenge. Julia didn't understand why it possessed her now. She felt *different*. The feeling had started during the holdup. When the bullet had entered Scott's brain, something dark had entered her brain as well. Yet her recognition of this didn't diminish her feelings of hate for the guy who had shot Scott. She *wanted* the darkness to remain with her, for now. It gave her strength.

Amy had indicated she knew something about her power. Amy believed Julia could heal Scott. It would have taken a demonstration of some kind to have given Amy such faith. What exactly had her mother shown Amy? *Why* had she shown her? Her mother did nothing without a reason, and to violate the Helpers' strict tradition of secrecy made no sense.

The eastern sky was turning from deep blue to faint yellow when Julia sat on her knees beside the pond. She faced east, in the direction of the light. The air was still. She sat for several minutes, waiting for the sun to peek above the treetops, and thought, if sunlight showed her distant places in the present and moonlight showed her the future, what would the glow of dawn reveal? Julia closed her eyes and took several deep breaths. Then she leaned over and gazed deep into the icy water.

Julia was confident of finding the hoods because of her previous experiences with normal sunlight viewing. She only needed to have the thought of someone to be shown his or her location. Sometimes she was drawn to a place where she could be of help. She had spotted the fire in the paper warehouse in such a manner.

Amy had been very perceptive to question her stumbling upon both the fire and Lieutenant Crawley

72

by accident. Of course, it was no accident. Once she drove to the warehouse and saw how the fire was expanding, she went straight to where she knew the nearest policeman was. She hadn't considered how Crawley would react to being caught with his mistress, although she did know ahead of time that he was having an affair. It was impossible to view the town and not bump into the two of them. Julia hadn't meant to pry, but if that cop didn't let up on her, he was going to be sorry. She could follow Crawley wherever he went. God knows what she could find out to use against him.

But leaning over the water in the present, Julia focused on a greater enemy.

Where are you, ugly butcher? Where is your greasy mustache and your fat friend? Show yourself. I want to show you something.

The water shone like hard steel slowly being heated. The sun would be up soon, but it was still a few minutes off. Julia felt herself sinking, faster than when she viewed in sunlight. Indeed, it almost felt as if she were falling headfirst into the pond. The vision hit with brutal clarity.

She was in the hospital, in intensive care, in the same hospital where Scott lay dying. Only Scott was not there. A motionless figure lay stretched out on a bed, covered with a sheet. Whoever it was— he or she must be dead. At the foot of the bed stood her mother. Behind her was the guy who had shot Scott.

You! Why are you with my mom?

He didn't have his mustache, but Julia knew it was him. She felt the hatred boil inside her. The jerk was cursing her mother now!

"You said you would help her!" he raved. "You lied to me. Look what you've done."

Her mother's eyes remained fastened on the figure beneath the sheet. "I'm sorry. I know you loved her. I loved her, too. She was very dear to me."

"You didn't even know her name! Get out of here. Get away from us. You should have left her alone. I hope you die."

Her mother looked pale and unsteady. But not as a result of what the guy said. She wasn't upset with him. She turned and touched his arm. "I wouldn't lie to you. I did know her. You see, I have this daughter—"

The guy threw off her hand. "Who's your daughter?"

Her mother watched him. "It doesn't matter."

"Who is she?" he demanded.

Her mother's eyes strayed to the figure on the bed. "Why do you want to know?"

The guy struck her mother in the face. Blood spurted from her nose over her white nurse's uniform. "You'll see why, witch! I saw your daughter's picture on your desk. I'm going to find her, and then you'll pay for what you did. You'll pay in blood."

Her mother wasn't afraid. She calmly removed a handkerchief from her pocket and pressed it to her nose. She spoke in a kind voice, as always. "I am responsible for everything I do. We all are. But there is still forgiveness. You have to forgive yourself, or you will pay for the rest of your life. It wasn't your fault, son."

The guy wouldn't listen to her. With one last look at the covered figure on the bed, he whirled around and stormed out of the room. Her mother stepped up to the head of the bed and put her hand on what had to

74

be the figure's head. Then she closed her eyes and began to cry softly.

Julia had never seen her mother cry.

Who is that dead person?

The hospital room vanished.

Julia sucked in a deep breath and became aware of her body again.

The rays of the rising sun had hit the water.

Julia looked into the pond again, still shaking from what she had seen and heard. Yes, what she had *heard*. Now she could hear as well as see. How could that be? She was given no time to reflect. Almost immediately, her vision was swept to a filthy garage. She was in the present now, she could tell. The sun peeked through the dirty window of the garage at the same angle it was shining on her pond. The two guys who had hit the gas station sat on the floor beside their motorcycles, smoking joints and drinking beer.

"Pretty smooth weed," the fat guy said.

"It takes the edge off the ice," the guy with the mustache agreed. Julia had read about ice—it was a powerful stimulant that was generally smoked. People who used ice went for days without sleeping. Prolonged use led to insanity.

Julia was surprised that the guy with the mustache was younger than she had thought. He could have been in high school still. He also wasn't so bad looking as she had thought. He did need a good bath and a shave, though. He looked as if he slept on top of an oil pan.

The fat guy coughed. "I don't know what's wrong with me," he complained.

The guy with the mustache chuckled. "You're a junkie. Only ice can make you feel nice."

The fat guy coughed some more, then spat on the garage floor. "Jesus!" he cried.

"What is it?"

"There's blood in my spit. I'm bleeding."

His partner was bored. "Then quit spitting."

"No, Frank. It's real blood. Damnit. I told you that redhead did something to me."

Frank. Frank what?

Frank snorted. "She didn't touch you. What are you talking about?"

"There was something spooky about her. That's all I know. Frank, I think I need a doctor. I don't feel so good. I can't see right."

Frank knocked the joint from his partner's hand. "You stay straight for a few hours and you'll see just fine. You're not going to any doctor. He'd take one look at you and call the police. That redhead you're complaining about saw us both." Frank took another puff of his joint. "She's out there, but I know where to find her."

"Why did you have to shoot that guy?"

"Because I didn't like the way he dressed."

The fat guy was worried. "I don't like this. We weren't going to shoot anybody. We could go to jail. Then what are we going to do?" He added, contradicting himself, "Why didn't you hit the girl, too, while you were at it?"

Frank smiled. "'Cause she put a move on me. She moved fast as lightning."

"How do you know her?"

"I saw her picture once."

The fat guy panted. "I can't breathe. She hurt my insides."

Frank slapped his partner on the side of the head.

"Shut up!" He jumped to his feet and paced beside the motorcycles. "We don't have time for this crap. We have a job to do tonight, and you better get straight by then. We got to get that bread to pay King. If you think you feel bad now, think about what King could do to you."

"I don't know if I'll be able to get on my bike tonight," the fat guy moaned.

"You won't have to go far. Down to the lake and back. It'll take us twenty minutes, tops. Then we can stop at King's, get rid of our debts, and buy more crystals. Then you'll feel all right."

The fat guy smiled weakly. "How much do you think we'll get?"

Frank took a small black book from a shelf near the bikes. "They didn't show me their books at the store," Frank said, studying notes or a diagram or something. "Barnes may be out in the boonies, but it's on a busy road. They got the business; they'll have the bread. I guarantee it."

"What time are we going?"

"At closing," Frank said. "Eleven o'clock."

That's all I need to know.

The stroke of incredible good luck upset Julia's concentration. Her vision wavered and then broke altogether. The garage disappeared. The pond shook with ripples. She realized her right hand was wet. She had subconsciously been reaching for the guy's neck and had touched the surface of the water.

Julia was about to stand up and return to Jim when another scene became visible in the pond. Because the water wasn't flat, her vision was far from clear. She saw enough, however, to know that a carload of old women all dressed in black was making its way up the road toward her house. There were six of them, and as Julia peered closer, the woman in the front near the window suddenly yanked her head around. It was as if their eyes locked over the distance that separated them. It was her aunt, and the woman was angry because she knew she was being watched. Julia immediately turned her vision aside, studying where the car was. The women were near Round Meadow—approximately ten miles from her house.

They'll get to my house in fifteen minutes. Even if Jim doesn't answer the door, my aunt will know he's inside.

Julia jumped up, feeling a rush. It was never wise to leap up out of a viewing session, but she didn't have time to worry about how she felt. She was in good shape. She could cover the mile to her house in six minutes. Throwing her long red hair over her shoulder, she set off at a hard pace. She knew now why she had felt someone trailing her.

What will they do to me?

Nothing. They wouldn't get near her. She wouldn't let them.

By the time she reached her house, she was gasping for air. A cramp as big as a cantaloupe had formed inside her liver. She had never run so hard in her life. It was all finally catching up with her: the grief, the stress. She hadn't slept in ages.

"Jim!" she called.

He burst out the back door. "What is it?"

"We have to get out of here. Do you have Scott's keys? Good—you drive. We have to go!"

"Why?"

Julia opened the car door. "Some people are after

me. I can't explain it right now. They'll be here in minutes."

Jim jogged over to the driver's side. "Did you find out about the guys who shot Scott?"

"Yeah. They're going to hit the liquor store on Barnes at eleven tonight. The one by the lake."

They got in the car and Jim started the engine. "How does your friend know this?" he asked, amazed.

"She owns a crystal ball."

"Huh?"

"Nothing. Hurry."

"What are we going to do?" Jim asked.

Julia glanced up the road as Jim backed the car out. There was no sign of them, but that didn't mean anything. Julia wondered if her aunt had a viewing technique of her own, and if she needed a pond.

If she looks into the future, she'll know exactly where I'm going tonight.

"Right now we're going to leave here as fast as we can," Julia answered Jim. "We'll find a motel somewhere. We have to rest."

"And then?"

"Then, later, we get ourselves a gun."

"They're really going to hit that liquor store?"

"No," Julia said. "*They're* going to get hit at that liquor store."

Chapter Six

AMY was in the hospital cafeteria drinking her sixth cup of coffee when the group of women in black passed by in the hall. It was eight o'clock in the morning; she knew if she didn't lie down soon she would black out where she sat. The women caught her eye, however, and not just because of their somber dress. One of them looked like Julia's aunt. Amy had met the woman at the memorial service for Mother Florence. She'd appeared completely unaffected by her sister's death. Julia had kept an obvious distance from her.

Amy set down her cup and went after them. She watched as the aunt—it was definitely her, Amy decided—stopped to question a nurse. The nurse pointed in the direction of Scott's room. The group of women had started off again when the aunt suddenly stopped and eyed Amy. The others pulled up behind her.

"Who are you?" she asked.

Amy took a halting step backward. The aunt was

bone thin; the lines of her jaw moved visibly as she spoke. She was also incredibly pale, and the hard wrinkles around her eyes looked as if they'd been carved. Her age was difficult to estimate. Amy would have said she was close to seventy, except for the energy that emanated from her. She approached Amy swiftly.

"You're Julia's friend," she said.

"Yes," Amy said. The woman's eyes were set deep, but they burned bright. Amy found it difficult not to be drawn into them.

"Where is Julia?" the aunt asked.

"I don't know."

"Who's with her?"

"My boyfriend."

"What's his name?"

"Jim."

"Jim what? Where does he live?"

Her eyes are hypnotizing. Look away. Look away.

Amy shook herself and glanced at the floor. "I don't know."

"You don't know your boyfriend's name?"

Amy glanced up, being careful not to focus on the woman. The aunt exuded a powerful presence. Amy was reminded of Mother Florence, except here there was little warmth, no softness.

"What do you want Julia for?" Amy asked.

The old woman tilted her head to the side. One of her companions—an old bag of bones if ever there was one—whispered a few words in the aunt's ear. The aunt nodded and briefly shut her eyes. When she reopened them, she was more relaxed, but distant. Amy found this even more disturbing.

"You were there last night when the boy was shot," she said.

"Yes," Amy said.

"What did Julia do?"

"Nothing."

"Didn't she try to stop the other boy from entering the place? The boy she is with now?"

"Yes. How do you know that? Have you talked to Julia?"

The aunt turned to her followers. They nodded grimly. "It's important we talk to her," the aunt said. "You know who I am?"

"Yes," Amy said. "But I told you, I don't know where she is."

"I need your boyfriend's name and number."

"I'm sorry. I can't give you that."

"Look at me, child."

"What for?"

"Look at me," the aunt repeated firmly.

Amy looked. She didn't want to, but she felt helpless to refuse. The aunt leaned closer, her pupils filling Amy's field of vision. The woman's eyes were violet, flawlessly clear, like a child's, just born into a world without shadows. They shifted in tiny circles—there was a dreamlike quality to the motion. Amy wondered if perhaps everything else in her surroundings was moving and the woman's eyes were the only things still. Suddenly Amy felt both reassured and confused, as if she were entering a forbidden land with someone who had been there many times before.

"Where is Julia?" the woman asked softly, rhythmically.

"She's with Jim," Amy heard herself say. "I don't think they're at his house."

82

"What are they doing?"

"They're going after the guys who shot Scott."

"How?"

"I don't know. Julia says she can find them."

"Why does Julia want to find them?"

"I think she wants to kill them."

Kill. Murder? Julia? No . . .

Amy blinked. What was she saying? The old woman was inside her head again! Amy backed up a step, pressing her butt against the wall. She raised an arm across her face. The woman remained where she was, regarding Amy thoughtfully. Her group of followers whispered darkly behind her.

"Thank you," the aunt said. "You've been helpful."

"You're not going to hurt her, are you?" Amy asked anxiously.

The aunt waved her hand. "It's no concern of yours." She turned to leave, her followers with her. Amy stood up straight.

"Wait," she called. "Can you help my friend?"

The aunt paused and glanced over her shoulder. "Who?"

"Scott. The one who got shot."

Sadness touched the woman's face. "Who?" she repeated, as if she'd heard correctly but was responding to a different question.

Amy didn't understand, and the aunt didn't explain. The group turned as one and headed in the direction of Scott's room. Amy wanted to follow them but had no strength in her legs.

It was then that Randy Classick walked up to her.

"I heard what happened," he said, giving her a hug. "I can't believe it. Good old Scott. He was the only one in the whole goddamn school who had any brains. There's no way I'm going to pass chemistry now."

Randy was being ridiculous, as usual, but Amy could see he was upset. In fact, he looked as if he'd just finished crying.

Out the corner of her eye, Amy watched the women in black swoop through the double doors at the end of the hall.

Why do they want to see him?

"He's still breathing," Amy said hopefully. "He might wake up. The doctors say that if he regains consciousness he stands a chance." She forced a chuckle that hurt deep inside her chest. "You don't have to fail chemistry."

"I hear he's in a coma."

"Yeah." She sniffed. *Coma*—the word sounded so empty. Randy put a hand on her shoulder.

"How're you doing, kid? You been here all night?" She nodded. "It's been a long night. What are you doing here?"

"I work here."

"You do? I didn't know that. What do you do?"

"Odds and ends. A little surgery, a little janitorial."

"Since when?"

"Since they hired me six months ago. I was working here when we went out. Don't you remember? I had that stethoscope. I tried to listen to your heart with it."

"That was your hand."

"Oh, yeah. Well, that was unprofessional of me." Randy paused and stared down the hall at intensive care. His big shoulders sagged. "This whole thing makes me feel sick. He was just going in for something to drink and they shot him?"

"Yeah. Julia was with him."

"I didn't know that. Is she all right?"

Amy nodded. "Yeah. One guy shot at her but missed."

"What kind of world do we live in? I hope Scotty wakes up."

"Randy? There's a group of old women dressed in black looking for Julia. Have you seen them?"

"Yeah. What do they want her for?"

"I'm not sure. One of them is her aunt, but I know Julia doesn't like her. I think they're trying to see Scott right now. Is there any way you could get in there and listen to what they're saying?"

"They won't get into intensive care unless they're family."

"I got in last night," Amy said.

"Yeah? Scott's parents must have told the nurses it was all right. But his parents have gone home. I met them in the parking lot when I came into work. That's who I heard the news from. I don't think you have to worry about those women hassling Scott."

"I told you, it's Julia I'm concerned about. I'm serious, Randy. They're spooky. I know that aunt can get in. She has a way about her—like she can hypnotize you—I can't really explain it. Could you go spy on her?"

"I'd have to put on a green gown and pretend I'm an orderly."

"What's wrong with that?"

"I hate wearing those things."

"Randy!"

"The nurses on duty might recognize me."

"They might not. Wear a bonnet. Wear a mask over your face. Do what it takes. I've got to know what the aunt wants Julia for." She took his hand. "Please? You told Julia if she ever needed help, to give you a call. Well, I think she needs help now."

"Will you go out with me if I do it?"

"Scott's lying inside dying and you're asking me out?"

Randy shrugged. "Scott was always for a guy getting it when he could."

Amy hit him. "You're disgusting! Yes, I'll go out with you. Get your gown on. Hurry."

Randy was gone three quarters of an hour. When he returned, he was wearing a white coat and a name tag that read "Dr. Bower, GYN-OB." The coat was too small for him, but he looked happy in it.

"What took you so long?" Amy asked.

"I was heading to intensive care when a frantic nurse grabbed me and asked me to examine a woman in labor."

"You're full of it!"

"I'm not kidding."

"What did you do?"

Randy shrugged. "Just put my hand on her belly and told her she was doing fine and that I'd be back when the baby came out."

Amy became impatient. "Did those women get in to see Scott?"

"You were right, yeah—two of them did. They were in intensive care when I arrived. One of them must have been Julia's aunt. She was talking about Julia's mother."

"What was she saying?"

"I didn't hear much of it. The nurse kept telling me I was in the wrong place. But the aunt said to her partners something about a girl who died in a motor-cycle accident a few months back. I got the impression Julia's mom took care of the girl."

"That's interesting." Amy remembered Mother Florence talking about the accident. It had been a couple of days before the stroke that killed her. The two of them had been sitting in her kitchen, drinking tea.

"She wasn't wearing a helmet, Amy. Her skull hit the pavement."

Amy remembered how Mother Florence's hand trembled when she raised the cup to her lips. She never said why, but Amy knew the death of this girl meant more to her than those of her other patients.

"Did the woman say anything else?" Amy asked.

"Yeah. Something about how the meddling had to be stopped."

"Who was she talking about then?"

"I don't know."

"I bet it was Julia."

"Wait a sec," Randy said. "I don't get this. Why does Julia have to be afraid of her own aunt?"

"The woman's weird."

"My mother's weird. So what?"

"I don't know, but I think the aunt blames Julia for what happened to Scott. She indicated as much when I spoke to her." Amy stopped for a moment, lost in thought. "Randy, there's something wrong with Julia. Since Scott got shot, she's had a wild look in her eyes. She wants to kill the guys who held up the station."

"I want to kill them. There ain't nothing strange about that."

"It's strange for Julia. I know her; she's not that way. Randy, you were working here when that girl died in the motorcycle accident. Do you know any-thing about it?"

"Nope. I don't pay any attention to the patients—they're all sick. They just depress me."

"Why do you work here, then?" Amy asked.

"The nurses are all horny. Hey, you know, I called that woman Scott had with him last night. She wants to make me dinner at her house."

"I'm happy for you. But we've got to talk about Julia. I think what happened last night has something to do with the girl who died in the motorcycle accident."

"Huh?" Randy said.

"The guys who hit the station were on motorcy-cles."

"Lots of guys ride bikes."

"Yeah, but Julia's aunt is here to see Scott and she's talking about the accident. Look, I know it's a flimsy connection, but I have to check it out. Randy, could you get the hospital records of the girl who died in that motorcycle accident?"

"They put all that junk on computer. There's no way we can get into the system here, even if I knew how to type. I'd need codes and crap like that. When was the accident?"

"Just before school got out. June fifth, June sixth—around there."

Randy frowned. "That's not very long ago. They could still have the actual records stored here." Randy glanced over his shoulder. "I can get you in the basement where they keep the stuff. But you'll have to look for the records yourself. I've got to deliver that baby."

"Gimme a break. You don't look old enough to be a doctor."

Randy fingered his bruised chin. "When I looked in the mirror this morning after last night's game, I thought I looked plenty old."

"You're a pervert. You shouldn't be touching a woman who's in labor."

"As long as she's not in stirrups, I don't see what's wrong with it."

Chapter Seven

THE records in the basement weren't filed by the date the patient had been admitted or treated but by the patient's last name and the name of the physician. The hospital did keep patient records on location for a year. During that time the records were supposed to be transferred onto computer disk. The hospital had two hundred beds and served four surrounding towns. When Randy led Amy into the basement, she gasped. There were literally thousands of records, and Amy had no idea where to begin looking. Fortunately, she'd be left alone to study them. Randy said hardly anyone ever went into the basement on weekends.

"I'll be back to help—if I get the chance," Randy said.

"Can you turn on the heat?" Amy asked, shivering. It was surprisingly cold, and there weren't even any windows.

"Yeah. I'll even get you some coffee."

Amy yawned. "I'll need it." She touched Randy's

arm as he started back up the steps. "And could you check on Scott?"

"Sure, Amy."

The lighting in the basement was poor. Amy had to grab a stack of records and carry it to a desk with a small gooseneck lamp. She had been worried that it would take her a few minutes with each form to understand what the patient was suffering. Luckily, the diagnosis was listed on the front of each record. Even so, walking back and forth with the stacks ate into her time. The hours slipped by. Randy brought her coffee and doughnuts, and bad news. Scott's condition was worse. His temperature had climbed a whole degree and his brain waves were faint. The doctors said to expect the worst—soon.

Four o'clock came and Randy finished work and finally joined her. By then Amy had begun to despair of finding anything on the girl. Her fatigue was like a sack of sand on her head. Randy made her take a break while he took her place. He said the woman upstairs was still in labor, but that her own doctor had arrived and didn't need help delivering the baby. Amy used that time to call Jim's and Julia's houses but didn't reach either of them. Jim's parents said he had told them he was assisting the police in finding the robbery suspects. Amy knew he was lying.

I have to set things right.

Amy returned to the basement and slumped on the floor near where Randy was working. Her eyes were swollen and dry.

"I think we're on a wild-goose chase here," Randy said.

"You can stop if you want," Amy muttered.

"No. I don't mind helping. It's just that when we do

find the girl's record, it's only going to say how banged up she was when they brought her in."

Amy closed her eyes, a wave of weariness pouring over her. "I suppose you're right. But I'd know her name. And I was thinking that if the aunt talked about the accident, and she was here to see Scott, and Julia was . . . I don't know what I'm talking about. I can't think anymore. I'll help you in a second—I've just got to sit here a moment."

"Amy?" Randy was saying. "Are you there?"

"What?" She opened her eyes with a start.

"You fell asleep."

"No I didn't. What time is it?"

"After six. You were snoring."

"Get off it! I don't snore. What's that you're holding?"

Randy opened the record in his hand. "It's not the girl's file, sorry. It's about a guy who got injured on his motorcycle last June. I thought he might have been driving the bike the girl was on. He tore up his knee pretty bad. They had to put twenty stitches in it. But he must have had a helmet on: there's nothing in here about head injuries. The hospital treated him and turned him over to the police."

"Why?"

"Because he was stinking drunk when they brought him in."

"Really?"

"It says so right here. But I bet the same doctor who treated this guy saw the girl. Emergency has only one doctor on duty late at night." Randy flipped open the report. "It was Dr. Fishman. I know the guy. He's an idiot."

Amy sat up. "But we can use his name to find the girl's records."

"Isn't that what I just said?"

"Let me see that folder." Randy handed her the file. Amy checked the patient name. "Frank Truckwater," she muttered.

"Does it ring a bell?"

"No." Amy stood. "Let's concentrate on Fishman's files."

Because of the doctor's name, they were able to go through the files quickly. Still, it was another hour before they came across the record of a girl who had been in a motorcycle accident. Amy found it. The date matched the one on Frank Truckwater's record.

The girl's name was Kary Florence.

"She has the same last name as Julia," Randy said, reading over her shoulder.

"I noticed."

"Do you think they're related?"

"No," Amy said. Then she reminded herself how the girl's death had devastated Mother Florence. "Well, I can't be sure. But this girl was only sixteen. Julia would have told me if she had a cousin."

"It's a hell of a coincidence that the aunt was talking about this chick. And then we find out she has the same last name as Julia," Randy said.

"Now you're beginning to sound like me." Amy scanned the record. On the night of June seventh at two-forty A.M., Kary Florence was admitted to the emergency room suffering from severe head injuries and internal bleeding. Several pages of technical information followed, the bottom line being that she had died three days later. She had revived only briefly from her initial comatose state. Amy remembered

Mother Florence saying the girl had woken up long enough to drink something and talk to her boyfriend.

"Sounds like she really got wasted," Randy said, reading along with her. Amy closed the report and pressed it to her chest.

"But what does it have to do with last night?" Amy raised her head. "What was that?"

Randy cocked his head. "You're being paged over the loudspeaker. Better hurry."

Amy dashed upstairs, taking Frank Truckwater's and Kary Florence's records with her. She picked up the first phone she saw. The hospital operator connected her to Jim.

"Where have you been?" she asked. "I've been trying to get you all day."

Jim spoke softly. "I'm with Julia. How's Scott?"

"Not good."

"How bad is 'not good'?"

"Real bad. He can die any minute. Where are you and Julia?"

"Not far."

"Where is 'not far'?"

"Julia told me not to tell anybody where we are."

"Is she there?"

"Yes. But she's sleeping." Jim added hesitantly, "We're in a motel."

Amy had to swallow. "What?"

"It's not like it sounds. Julia thinks someone's after her. I don't know why."

"Someone *is* after her."

Jim was surprised. "Really? Who?"

"Her aunt—her aunt's clan. They were here at the hospital this morning."

94

"That's odd," Jim said thoughtfully. "How does Julia know these things?"

"What things?"

"Nothing," Jim said quickly.

"What things? Does she know who the guys are that shot Scott?"

"I can't talk about it."

Amy was suddenly upset. "Why can't you talk about it? You're my boyfriend. She's my best friend. You didn't even meet her until last night, and now you're sharing secrets and motel rooms with her. Let me talk to her. I don't want to talk to you anymore."

"I told you, she's sleeping."

"Then wake her up."

"I don't think that's a good idea," Jim said. "She's been under a lot of stress."

"What about me? I haven't even gone to bed yet. What's going on, Jim? Why did you call? To say goodbye? It won't be the first time, you know. All my boyfriends end up falling in love with Julia."

"I'm not in love with Julia."

Amy closed her eyes and leaned against the wall. "Are you still in love with me?" she asked quietly.

"I can't talk about stuff like that right now."

Amy wanted to swallow but she couldn't. The lump in her throat prevented her.

He's not saying yes. He's only saying yes to her.

"That's OK," she whispered.

"Look, Amy, I've got things to do. I just wanted to tell you that I'm all right and that I'll see you soon."

Her sorrow was painful. She felt as if she had lost him already. Yet her sense of loss felt darker than anything she had experienced before. Like the loss was forever.

"Jim, listen to me. Get away from Julia. Go home."

"I can't."

"Jim, I'm afraid. Please do this for me."

"What are you afraid of?"

"Remember last night? Julia got upset the second she met you. She was worried about *you,* not Scott. It was *you* she stopped from going into the gas station."

"So what?"

"You said it yourself. Julia knows things. But she doesn't know everything. You've got to wake her. I've got to talk to her. There's this guy. His name's Frank—"

"Did you say Frank?" Jim asked, amazed.

Oh, no. She must have come back. Randy said they left hours ago.

The aunt was standing alone at the far end of the corridor, near the flight of stairs that led to the basement. Amy could feel the power of the woman's eyes on her. Amy knew immediately the aunt had overheard every word she said to Jim, and probably everything she and Randy discussed while searching through the files.

She's the one who's been spying on us.

"I've got to go," Amy told him. "Call me back in a few minutes."

"Who's Frank?" he asked.

"Why?" she whispered. "Did Julia talk about him?"

Jim's wall went right back up. "No."

"She did. I can tell."

"No," Jim said.

"We have to talk about this. Call me in ten minutes."

"I can't."

"Jim!"

"I'm sorry." He paused. "You're a great girl, Amy. I always thought that."

Her heart was breaking. She knew it was hopeless. He wasn't going to disobey Julia, his princess. "Yeah. Thanks. Just take care of yourself, OK?"

"I will. I promise."

Amy set the phone down. She considered confronting the aunt, but no sooner did the thought cross her mind than the aunt disappeared out a side entrance. The woman could move. Amy dashed down the hallway but could find no sign of her. She hurried back to the basement. Randy was cleaning up the mess they had made.

"Forget that," she said. "We've got work to do. Julia and Jim are going after the guys who shot Scott."

"Does this mean you're no longer dating Jim and can concentrate on me exclusively?"

"Would you stop that! This is serious."

"How do they know who shot Scott?" Randy asked.

"I don't know. They just know. The whole world's going crazy. Look, I think Julia's aunt's been spying on us. I'm more sure than ever that she and her brood are out to get Julia. We've got to stop them."

"Does the aunt know who shot Scott?"

"Probably."

Randy shook his head. "What did those idiots do last night? Take out an ad in the paper? What do you want me to do?"

"Get in your truck and follow those women. Keep them away from Julia at all costs."

"Where is Julia?" Randy asked.

"I don't know."

"How am I supposed to keep them away from her then?"

"You're big. You're strong. Use your imagination." Amy grabbed his arm and dragged him toward the stairs. "You have to hurry. They're leaving now."

"What are you going to do?"

Julia must have mentioned the name Frank for Jim to have reacted the way he did.

Her parents had brought her car over and parked it in the hospital lot. Amy pointed to the records under her arm. "I'm going to visit the Florences and then the Truckwaters."

Chapter
Eight

JULIA didn't know it was a dream. Few dreamers do.

She was swimming naked with Scott in a Tahitian lagoon. The water was nectar, the sky heavenly. The surrounding tropical forest smelled of paradise, and they were happy.

"Julia, watch this!" Scott called, diving off a moss-covered boulder beside a delicious green waterfall. He cut through the water with barely a splash and resurfaced excited. "There's something down there!"

"What is it?" she asked, swimming over. The clear water sparkled jewel-like in the blazing sun. She could see their brown legs treading water, keeping them afloat. But the lagoon was deep—the bottom was hidden from view.

"It's a secret treasure. Should I get it for you?"

She smiled. "Sure."

Scott dived beneath the surface, his feet kicking in the air. A moment later Julia let out a squeal. He had pinched her bare butt!

"Got it," Scott said, his head poking back up.

"Some secret treasure," she said, laughing. "You can do better than that."

He was interested. "I can?"

She splashed him. "You're a naughty boy."

"Gimme a kiss," he said, paddling closer.

"No."

"Why not?"

"You have to give me a real treasure first." She pointed down. "Swim to the bottom. Get me something nice."

Scott was smiling, yet he looked doubtful, too. "How do you know there's anything down there?"

"I know." And she did. She always knew what lay hidden beneath the surface of a pond. She was a witch. She had magical powers. Of course, this was a lagoon. It was bigger. It connected to the ocean. It was a more dangerous pool to play in. It was for big girls only. Big boys. Scott was interested in her dare.

"What are you going to give me besides a kiss?" he asked.

"My love."

He was *very* interested. "All of it?"

She giggled. "All you can handle."

"It's a deal." He offered his hand, and she shook it. Then he took a deep breath. "I'll be back soon to collect my reward."

Scott dived under. Julia waited for him to return. Actually, she knew there was nothing on the bottom. They were in Tahiti. All he was going to find was sand—or, at best, a piece of coral.

Scott had been gone only a few seconds when Julia noticed how dark it had become. She was puzzled that she couldn't find the sun at all. That was odd, she thought. It had been high in the sky just a minute ago. Now there was only the moon. Staring straight overhead, Julia wondered at its reddish color. It was as if Mars were orbiting the earth instead of the moon.

"Scott?" Julia called. "Scott?"

The surface of the lagoon glittered with strange light from the strange moon, making it appear to be one vast pool of blood. The seconds turned into minutes. Julia began to panic.

"Scott! Come back, Scott!"

Bubbles began to break the surface all around her, millions of bubbles. She could have been swimming in a pot of boiling, bloody broth. Indeed, the water temperature was rising swiftly. She could feel her naked flesh burning, blistering.

"Scott!" she screamed.

No answer. There was nothing she could do. She had to save herself. She had to swim to the shore. She couldn't dive down after him. The water was scalding now. If she put her head under, she felt as if her face would melt off. Nothing could be more horrible. Then she would look like a witch, and everyone would recognize her for what she was.

Julia swam frantically toward the shore. It seemed to take forever before her feet touched the rough sand beneath the water. She stumbled onto the shore, gasping for air and crying in pain. Why was this happening?

Something broke the surface behind her.

"Julia!" Scott screamed, thrashing in the center of the lagoon.

Something had ahold of him. It could have been a shark. It could have been a monster. Scott's flesh was bloody, as if a dozen razors had sliced him from head to foot. His blood soaked into the frothy water as the bubbles grew in size and number around his flailing limbs. They broke the surface like the spewing gases of an erupting volcano. The stench in the air was unbearable—poisonous sulfur fumes.

"Julia!" Scott cried, before the thing yanked him back under. It was a sin against God, Julia knew, but she prayed for him not to resurface. She prayed for a quick death for him.

God did not listen to her prayer.

"Julia!" screamed Scott, coming up once more. This time it looked as if whatever had Scott was losing its hold on him. Scott was closer to the shore now, and his arms were free and struggling back to the shore. Frantic, Julia looked around for a rope. Surprised, she found one lying in the sand at her feet. It was silver and cold to the touch. It was too short to reach Scott from where she stood. Julia realized that if she was to have any chance of saving Scott, she would have to wade back into the boiling lagoon.

"Help me!" Scott pleaded, his right shoulder open, the bleeding muscle clearly visible.

"Hold tight!" she called, making a decision. "I'll save you."

Julia wrapped the cord around her waist and hurried into the water, letting out a cry as it heated up her already burned skin. She went halfway between Scott and the shore. Even there she was unable to see what had ahold of him. The rope coiled in her hands, she let loose with a mighty throw aimed toward his outstretched hands. She was lucky. He caught it on her first try. She began to pull him to safety.

But immediately she ran into a problem.

"Wait," she said. "Stop!"

The monster had regained its hold on Scott. It was pulling him back under, and terrified, Julia realized it was dragging her along with him. She forgot about saving her friend. She fought to untie the rope from her waist, unsuccessfully—for now it was in knots and tearing into her waist.

"No!" she screamed. "Let go of it, Scott! Let go of the rope!"

Scott couldn't hear her. He was too scared. He was also a goner. A hand with knives for nails reached up from the bubbling cauldron and caught hold of his forehead. Scott went under, and then the hand reappeared on a foaming red wave with Scott's torn flesh and the silver rope twisted between its gleaming nails.

It began to pull Julia toward it.

Julia screamed and screamed again.

"Julia. Julia, snap out of it."

Julia sat bolt upright in bed. The claws had ahold of her! Still trapped in her nightmare, she struck out with her right arm. Jim caught her fist an inch from his nose. She saw him, but she didn't recognize him. She thought he was going to bite her.

"No," she moaned.

"You were having a bad dream," he said. "It's over."

Realization hit suddenly, followed by a flood of relief. Julia's head fell against his chest, her heart pounding like a pneumatic drill. She was literally soaked with sweat.

"Oh, God," she whispered.

Jim's arms went around her, and she let herself melt

into them. She had never really had a boy hold her before. She realized she had always kept them at a distance—even Scott—because she felt none of their strength could equal her inner power. She was an egomaniac, she decided then. She was fooling herself about her power. One little dream and she was shaking like a leaf.

"You'll be all right in a minute," Jim said gently.

Julia sat back, wiping at her face, embarrassed. "I feel all right now. Thanks."

Jim let go of her. "It must have been a hell of a dream. You were thrashing around on the bed. I was worried what the people in the next room were going to think."

Julia nodded. "It was like being in hell." She added, "I was dreaming about Scott and me."

Jim lowered his head. "Were you two ever involved?"

"Not romantically. We grew up together. He **was** my best friend. He and Amy."

He was? He is! He's still alive.

Why did she have no hope?

Jim raised his head. "I talked to Amy a few minutes ago."

"How?"

"I called the hospital and had her paged. She hadn't gone home yet."

The question stuck in her mouth, and she had to force it out. "How's Scott?"

Jim shook his head. "Amy says he's worse."

"I see."

"Amy wanted to know where we were, what we were doing. I didn't tell her." Jim shrugged. "I don't think we know what we're doing."

"You can go home if you want, Jim."

"I will if you will."

"Don't you want to get those guys still?" she asked.

"Do you?"

Julia paused and rubbed her eyes. "I want something. I'm not sure what it is. I think I want someone to explain what's wrong with me."

"One of your best friends is dying because of a senseless, violent act. That's your problem."

She put down her hands. "But I feel *consumed*. Like if I don't get the guy, no one will ever get him. It started the instant I saw Scott get shot. Something snapped inside." She struggled for the right words. "And since then all I feel is hate. And I'm not like this." She shook her head. "But I must be like this."

Jim looked uncomfortable. "Julia, who did you go to see when you hiked into the woods?"

"I told you."

He caught her eye. "I'm afraid I don't believe in people with crystal balls—especially ones who live in forests."

She met his gaze. "Do you think my information's wrong?"

"No. That's the problem. I think you're right. Amy indirectly confirmed what you said."

Julia sat up. "What did she say?"

"She mentioned Frank."

"Frank? Did she say what his last name was?"

"I didn't ask. I don't know how Amy got his name. She was talking on a phone at the hospital when something interrupted her. It might have been your aunt."

"My aunt?"

"Yeah. Amy wanted me to call her back. She said your aunt is after you."

Julia nodded. "That's no surprise."

"It is to me, Julia. That's what confuses me. How do you know they're following you? How do you know who shot Scott? Why did Amy insist you touch Scott's wound? Why did I begin to feel like I was floating when you touched my neck?"

"I didn't know you had all those questions in your head."

"I'm not stupid."

"I know you're not." Julia shook her head. "But you don't believe in crystal balls. So what can I say?"

"Just tell me the truth."

"I can't."

"Why not?" Jim asked.

"You wouldn't believe me."

"Julia."

"No, Jim." She took his hand. "It's better this way. Trust me. Some things can't be talked about. You know that."

He was disappointed. But he squeezed her hand and nodded his head. "I know I can't talk about you."

"What do you mean?"

He stared at the window, but because the curtains were drawn he saw nothing. Julia had only a vague idea where they were. They had driven for about thirty miles after leaving her house.

"I can't talk about the way I feel about you," he said.

Julia was touched, but she wasn't surprised by his confession. She had noticed the way he was looking at her. Plus a minute more and she would have made the same confession. Her life had gone insane in the last twenty-four hours, but somehow she had managed to find the time to develop a crush on the boy in her vision.

Maybe that's why I saw him in the moonlight. I knew I would want to see him for many future days.

Julia reached out and threaded her fingers in his hair. "You're neat. Did anyone ever tell you that?"

There was no joy in his reply. "Amy tells me that all the time."

Julia's pain came at her from too many directions. "She's one of my best friends."

"She is my best friend."

"She told me." Julia continued to play with his hair. It was not soft and fine like hers, but thick and wild. She added sadly, "It sounds like soon I'm going to need another friend."

"It wasn't your fault."

"Yeah."

"There's nothing you can do."

Julia stared off into space, her skin hurt all over with what could have been a bad sunburn, except on her head, where a cold current seemed to pass through the very center of her brain. She let go of Jim's hair.

"In my nightmare, I was swimming with Scott in a lagoon," she said softly. "I told him to bring me a treasure from the bottom. I don't know what I expected—maybe I wanted you. Maybe I traded you for him. He died. The monster came and got him. Then it got me, too. We both died."

"It was just a dream."

"I don't just have 'dreams,' Jim. I see things."

"What kind of things?"

Julia shook herself. "Nothing."

"I fell asleep a little after you. I had a dream of my own. Would you like to hear it?"

"Sure."

Jim reached out to turn the switch on the lamp beside the bed. Julia glanced at a nearby clock. It was a quarter after seven and fairly dark in the room. The lamp was broken, and the light didn't go on.

"I was a spirit," Jim said. "I was at a football game between your school and mine. I sat in the stands beside you and Amy and Scott. Nobody knew I was there except you. You could see me. But when I tried to talk to you, you leaned over and whispered for me to be quiet, to keep our secret. It was like you didn't want me to tell other spirits that there was a mortal who knew about us."

Julia smiled. "That's a pretty dream."

"It was neat. I hated to wake up."

Julia lost her smile. "Jim, how have you felt since Scott got shot? I mean, other than being upset about his condition?"

Her question caught him off guard. "It's funny you should ask that. I've felt out of place. I look at the world, and it seems the same, but—it's like I can see *through* it. Nothing's real to me anymore. Does that make sense?"

Julia didn't like the sound of what he was saying.

He's not supposed to be here. It's true.

"It'll pass," she said.

"I'm sure it will. What are we going to do now?"

Julia thought of Frank cursing her mother and slapping her mother's face. She thought of Frank boasting in his garage about how he was going to get her next. More than ever, Julia decided, she wanted revenge.

"How old are you?" Julia asked.

"Eighteen."

"Good. You're going to buy me a rifle at the sporting-goods store in Darling Mall."

"That's over an hour from here."

"Then we'd better get going. They'll be open till nine."

"What are we going to do with these guys when we catch them?"

"We'll deal with that when it happens," she said vaguely, knowing very well what she was going to do. "All I can guarantee is that they'll be at the liquor store on Barnes Road at eleven o'clock."

Jim considered. "Maybe we could place them under citizens' arrest until the police get there."

"I don't want to call the police until after we have them. Lieutenant Crawley will probably just let them get away. He's such a klutz." She leaned closer. She was only seventeen. The sporting-goods store would want to see I.D. She *had* to take Jim with her. "What about the rifle?"

"We can get it. But I want to buy two of them."

Julia shook her head. "You're not coming into the liquor store with me."

"Right. I'm going to sit in the car while you risk your life. Gimme a break, would ya?"

Julia saw, of course, that to ask for his help meant to ask for all of it.

Images of a red-soaked moon came back to haunt her. She wondered if he was the last person in the world she should be asking for help.

The vision's over. It happened. It won't come around again.

But she didn't convince herself.

"All right," she said, gesturing to his red letterman's jacket. "But we're also buying you another jacket when we get the guns. The jacket you're wearing stands out like an emergency flag. There's no sense in making yourself such an easy target."

Chapter Nine

WHICH house to go to first wasn't difficult for Amy to choose. The Florences lived about halfway between the hospital and the Truckwaters. She didn't consider calling ahead to announce her visit.

"Hi, I wanted to talk to you about your dead daughter." Or *"Hi, did you shoot my friend last night?"*

The Florence residence was located in a town approximately twenty miles south of Indian Pole called Wine. Wine was slightly larger than Indian Pole, and Wine's houses were bigger and more extravagant. On the average, they had four bedrooms instead of three, and their chimneys were usually straighter. Nevertheless, Amy was surprised to find that the Florence residence was practically a mansion. Amy didn't know anyone who was rich. Parking at the end of the long driveway, she approached the tall dark wood front door with apprehension.

A red-haired gentleman with beautiful green eyes answered.

"May I help you, young lady?"

He has Julia's eyes!

"Are you Mr. Florence?"

"Yes."

"Hi, my name's Amy Belle." She offered her hand, and he shook it after a slight hesitation. There was a light on behind him and a stereo was playing softly, but Amy could see no one else behind him. "This is sort of hard to explain. I've come about your daughter, Kary."

The man stiffened. "Did you know Kary?"

"No, we never met."

"Then what is it you want?"

"I was at the hospital today. My friend's been shot in the head and I was waiting for him to wake up." She paused. She should have rehearsed this. "I happened to see your daughter's medical record—"

"You saw my daughter's medical record?" he interrupted. "How is that—"

"It's a long story. My friend got shot by a guy who rides a motorcycle. I was wondering if your daughter used to go with a guy who rode a bike?"

Anger flashed in the man's eyes. "What kind of questions are these? Get out of here before I call the police." He started to shut the door. Amy stopped him with her hand.

"Wait! I've also come to talk to you about Julia."

The man stopped. He let the front door swing back open. "Do you know Julia?" he asked.

"I'm her best friend. Are you her dad?"

He was stunned. "How did you know that?"

"I didn't know until just now. When was the last time you saw Julia?"

"At her mother's memorial service."

112

"I was there," Amy said. "I didn't see you."

"No one saw me. I didn't go inside the church."

"Why? You were married to Mother Florence once, weren't you?"

"Yes. But that's a long time ago and a long story. How is Julia?"

"She's in trouble. She's trying to track down the guys who shot our friend. She's got a lead on them, but she won't take it to the police. She's also got her aunt and her aunt's friends on her tail."

The man spoke gravely. "I'm acquainted with her aunt."

"Who is she? I met her at the hospital and it was like she . . . I don't know how to say it."

"Like she could control you?" the man asked.

"Yes. How does she do it?"

"You knew Julia's mom? Well?"

"Yes."

"Then you must know that she was a very special woman. The aunt and her friends are like that, too—special."

"But Mother Florence was the nicest woman in the world. These ladies are spooky."

The man nodded. "But all the women have things in common. Trust me."

"What are they? Can they heal like Mother Florence could?"

The man raised an eyebrow. "She told you that? I'm surprised."

"Julia can heal, too."

A look of wonder crossed his face. "Really?"

"Maybe not like Mother Florence, but she can do it. Look, can I ask a real personal question?"

"You may. I may not answer it, though."

"How come Julia never talks about you? Does she ever see you?"

The man stopped to think. A weight seemed to descend upon him then. When he finally spoke, it was in an uncertain voice. "Julia doesn't know me. I left Elizabeth—Mother Florence, as you call her—shortly before Julia was born."

"Why?"

"It was personal."

"Did the family scare you?"

She had hit near the mark. The man shook once before quickly mastering himself. "I should say I scared myself. Elizabeth was too fine for someone like me."

Amy spoke delicately. "Kary was your daughter, too?"

"Yes," he said briskly. "I'm sure you looked at her birth date."

He cheated on Mother Florence. Did he run away out of guilt?

"I'm not trying to be nosy. I'm just trying to help Julia. Did you talk to Mother Florence when Kary died?"

It was painful for him. "Just before."

"Did Mother Florence know Kary was your daughter?" Amy asked.

"Yes. I went to Elizabeth."

"Why?"

He shrugged. "I think you know why."

He wanted her to heal Kary! It was he who asked her.

"Mother Florence died only a few days after that," Amy said.

114

"I know. It was a great tragedy."

"Can you tell me anything about Frank Truck-water?"

"Why do you think Frank is responsible for the shooting of your friend? Not that I would be surprised. Frank was a rotten kid when Kary was alive, and when she died he turned to poison. He's a drug addict and a thief. If Julia's after him, I hope she kills him."

There was real venom in his voice. "What if he kills Julia?" Amy asked. "She's your daughter, for godsakes."

"I know it will sound strange for a father to say this, but I'm not worried about her. The women in that family have a way of taking care of themselves."

"Mother Florence never took enough care of herself."

The man nodded gravely. "I remember." He added, "But if Julia wants Frank, she'll get him."

"How can you be sure?"

"Her mother told me some things about Julia. Nothing about her healing abilities, but other things. I'm her father, after all, and Elizabeth did respect that."

"What did she tell you?"

"You say you're Julia's best friend. You ask her when you see her. I'll let her decide what you should know."

"Where does Frank Truckwater live? I got his address from his hospital record, but I don't know if it's current."

"I have no idea," the man said.

Amy scratched her head. "Maybe it doesn't matter.

I don't even know if Frank is the right guy. Do you have a picture of Frank? Of him and Kary together? I wasn't in the station when my friend was shot. I didn't see who did it. But I listened closely to the descriptions Julia gave the police."

"Any picture we had of Frank was destroyed the day I buried Kary."

"You really hate him?"

"He was drunk when he had the accident with my daughter. As far as I'm concerned, he murdered her."

The conversation sort of died right there. Amy couldn't think of anything else to ask. Plus she was anxious to get to Frank Truckwater's house before it got any later. It was already near nine.

"Thank you for your time, Mr. Florence," she said. "I'm sorry to intrude on you like this." She turned to leave.

"Wait. Amy, is it? Could you give Julia a message for me?"

"Sure."

"Tell her I'd like to meet her, if she wants to meet me."

Amy smiled. "I know that'll make her happy."

"What's the name of your friend who's been shot?"

"Scott Hague."

"Is he in bad shape?"

"He was shot in the head."

The man grimaced. "I'm sorry to hear that. Was he a close friend of Julia's?"

"The three of us grew up together."

The man blinked. "You might want to keep Julia away from him."

"Why?"

116

"You get nothing for free in this world. Did you know that, Amy?"

"I suppose. But I'm not sure I understand you."

Mr. Florence did not explain further. "I'm sure it was just a coincidence," he muttered. "Goodbye, Amy."

"Thanks again."

Chapter Ten

RANDY Classick had followed the old women to a motel where they went inside. A couple of hours passed and it got dark and Randy got cold. He began to wonder what the hell he was doing. He really liked Amy, and he was in awe of Julia, but he couldn't see how he was helping either of them by sitting in his truck and eating peanuts. Whenever he was bored, he ate. That was the reason he was as big as he was. School bored him. His job bored him. Even football bored him now. He doubted they were ever going to win a game with the idiot of a coach they had. So he ate.

Randy put another whole peanut into his mouth and spit out the shell on the floor of his truck. He made no bones about being a slob. If he enjoyed a meal, he belched, and he didn't care if everybody heard it. But he didn't consider himself crude or a slob. He had principles. For example, he always took a shower before he went out with a girl. He may not have been movie-star handsome, but he tried to look the best he could—within limits. He would never go on a diet for any girl. He could swear to that. Once while eating at a fast-food joint, a girl from school suggested that one shake was enough for him. The nerve. He took her advice. He poured his second shake over her head and just drank the first. Yeah, he was flexible when it came to girls. As long as they didn't tell him what to do.

He was worried about Scott, though. He liked Scott. The dude could make him laugh. He was also smart. Randy appreciated intelligence. If Scott hadn't got shot in the head, Randy would have laid odds he would've become another Steven Spielberg or George Lucas. But Randy didn't want to bet on Scott's chances now. He'd seen Scott in intensive care while he'd been shadowing those old women. Randy had seen mannequins that looked healthier.

Hey, God, if my buddy's going to die, let him die tonight. I can't work at that place knowing he's rotting in intensive care.

Randy dropped his bag of peanuts and slid down in the seat to hide. He peeked out the side window. The old women were coming out of the motel, six of them now, led by that skeleton-faced aunt of Julia's. She looked like a cardboard figure left over from a Halloween display. He was sure they were members of a Satanic cult. He bet they killed little puppies and burned Bibles. Randy had never read the Bible himself, but he did like dogs.

He watched as the women piled into their old station wagon and pulled out of the parking lot. Randy knew something about following people. He'd read a lot of spy novels and knew he didn't have to keep them in sight at all times, just as long as he saw where they turned. He fired up his truck and let the women get a hundred yards ahead before he moved onto the road.

Randy had a piece of garbage for a vehicle—literally. He had found the truck at the dump. Someone had driven it in at night and left it for the rats. The guy at the dump said he could have it for free if he could get it out of there, which he did with the help of a couple of guys on the team. It was Scott who had helped him rebuild the engine. Scott was amazing—he could understand the directions in auto-mechanic books, which could have been written in Japanese, as far as Randy was concerned.

But the truck wasn't great. It groaned and heaved as Randy tried to keep up with the women. He didn't know what he was going to do, not really. Amy had told him to keep the women away from Julia at all costs. What could he do? Ram them off the road? He wasn't a violent person. He didn't even own a gun, and the only reason he kept a knife in his truck was for carving trees.

Randy loved trees. He loved how they stood there year after year without bothering anybody. But trees could get kind of boring, too, he thought, when they all looked alike. So he gave them a little individual personality by putting faces on them. He figured if Scott died, he'd sneak onto campus at night and put Scott's face on a tall pine just outside the window of the girls' showers. He'd put a grin on old Scott's face, and they'd both know what he was grinning about.

The women were heading out of town when they suddenly pulled into a gas station. Randy approached within a couple of hundred yards, hugging the edge of the road, and studied them. The station was a self-serve, but the way they sat and waited for help, Randy wondered if they knew what a self-serve was. A brilliant idea popped into his head right then—brilliant because he averaged only one halfway decent idea a year. This idea looked like it would work. Quickly he swung his truck behind the gas station and jogged over to the women's car. It was a cold night—his breath came out in small white puffs.

The aunt was behind the wheel. Randy almost changed his mind about his brilliant idea when she glanced up at him. He'd heard the expression *piercing eyes* before, but this was the first time he had ever felt dissected by someone's glance. The violet in her eyes burned with a cold light. Then he decided that if this was the woman Amy asked him to keep away from Julia, then he'd better damn well do it. Randy's respect for Julia knew no bounds.

"What can I do for you ladies tonight?" he asked.

"We'd like our gas tank filled, please," the aunt said.

"Regular unleaded or super unleaded?"

"Regular unleaded."

Randy had only two bucks on him. He'd need time to do what he planned—he needed the gas running while he worked. He glanced at the guy inside the gas station who took the money. The guy was busy with another customer.

"Could you pay first?" he asked. "It's station policy."

The aunt stared at him. "Do you work here?"

Randy chuckled. "I practically live here, lady."

The aunt hesitated, then gave him a crisp twenty. Randy hurried to the cash register. "Fill it up on six," he said. "Unleaded."

The customer had left. The guy behind the window nodded and continued reading a *Playboy*.

Randy got the gas going, then casually strolled by the aunt's window. "Look under the hood?" he asked.

"That's not necessary," she said.

"I don't know about that," he remarked. "I thought I saw steam coming from under your hood when you pulled into the station. I better check the fluid level in your radiator."

"I didn't see any steam," the aunt said.

"That's what you got us for. I'll just give it a quick look if you'll pop the hood."

Again, the woman hesitated before doing as he asked. When Randy had the hood up, he quickly scanned the engine. Ordinarily, the best way to disable a car was to swipe the distributor cap. But he didn't have his jacket to hide it in, and he doubted that the needle-eyed hag was going to let him walk off with it sticking out of his pocket. Randy decided to take the points, which were located inside the distributor cap. He was able to pop it open with his finger. Ordinarily the sabotage should have taken him thirty seconds to complete, but he didn't have a light, and he was sweating. The gas was through pumping before he had the points in his pocket and the distributor cap back on. The total came to fifteen dollars and eighty-nine cents. He slammed down the hood and took the pump nozzle out of the tank.

"How is the radiator?" the aunt asked.

"Looks OK to me. Wait here. I'll get your change."

Randy jogged to the window. The man had his change waiting, and Randy didn't mind pocketing the four dollars and eleven cents.

"Thanks, buddy," he told the guy. "Check out the

babe on page ninety-eight. She was built for cold Idaho nights."

Randy walked around the back of the station and got in his truck, and drove away. He could see the women in his rearview mirror, glancing around for him. He would have liked to stop and watch them from a distance when they couldn't start their station wagon, but he was starting to worry about Amy. She had said she was going to see the Florences and the Truckwaters, and he knew she suspected the Truckwater dude of shooting Scott. Randy decided he would head out there instead of going back to the hospital. Unknown to Amy, he had memorized Truckwater's address. He didn't have much of a head for numbers, but there hadn't been many numbers to it:

19 Folkshome Road, Derrel.

Randy checked the time—nine-twenty. He'd be there in half an hour, if he didn't have to stop for gas. He had less than a quarter tank left. His truck guzzled fuel. He was glad he now had six bucks instead of two.

Chapter Eleven

JULIA and Jim reached the mall ten minutes before closing. They had to run to the sporting-goods store. The man who worked there, however, was happy to help them. Retired from the police force for a dozen years, there was nothing he liked better than to talk about guns. His name was Barker. Of course, right away he asked them what they wanted the guns for: hunting bird, deer, rabbit, shooting cans, protection.

"Protection," Julia said. "What would be better, a rifle or a shotgun?"

Barker scratched his tan, leathery, crewcut head. "Ordinarily you'd want a pistol or revolver; something you could put in the desk drawer beside your bed."

"But isn't there a waiting period for buying a handgun?" Jim asked.

"Yes," Barker said. "There is a form that has to be filled out. We check whether you've been convicted of a felony, things like that. But you can usually pick up the weapon within two weeks.'

"That's no good," Julia said quickly. "We need a gun tonight. Two of them."

"Somebody hassling you, young lady?" Barker asked, giving her a shrewd look. He was not an idiot like Lieutenant Crawley. He could see she was tense.

"Yes," Julia said.

"If that's the case, you might be better going to the police," Barker said. "They know how to use their guns, and they know when not to use them."

Julia forced a smile. "We're not trigger-happy, sir. I mainly want it to feel safe. You understand. I'm sure I'll never fire it."

"How old are you?" Barker asked.

"Eighteen," Julia lied. She turned to Jim. "But my boyfriend's buying the guns. He's eighteen, too."

"I have I.D," Jim said.

"You'll need I.D. and money," Barker said, leading them to a rack of weapons. "If you're buying this for protection, I'd recommend a shotgun. It doesn't require the accuracy of a rifle." Barker picked up a shotgun and handed it to Jim. "That's a Remington twelve-gauge pump action. There are two main types of shotguns—pumps and semiautomatics. Pumps are usually the kind you see on TV. You have to pump before you fire. With semiautomatics you just pull the trigger."

"How many shots can this fire before you have to reload?" Julia asked.

"Five," Barker said. "You can get an extended tube that will give you more shots. But you'd find that unnecessary for most purposes."

Jim handed Julia the shotgun. It was surprisingly heavy. She had never used a gun in her life. Her mother had said that people who bought weapons for protection were like people who went to Las Vegas to make money.

"When you sit down at any gambling table, you have to understand that the house has the advantage. In the long run, you are bound to lose."

Julia had asked her to explain, but her mother's answer was as abstract as her analogy was confusing. Her mom felt that the fear that drove people to buy guns drew violence to them like magnets.

"You get two things in life, Julia—what you really want and what you really fear. This may not seem true to you now but it's always the case. Always."

Julia sometimes wondered if her mother had wished for an early death.

Julia wondered what *she* secretly wished for.

"It sounds like a semiautomatic would be better if you only have to pull the trigger," Julia said.

Barker shook his head. "Most policemen prefer a pump action. There are less things that can go wrong. A pump action won't jam on you. Also, they're cheaper. This shotgun here runs two fifty. A semiautomatic would cost you another hundred. Remington's a solid brand. You're holding the first gun I ever bought my daughter, young lady."

"How old was she when you gave it to her?" Julia asked.

"Ten. She's thirty now, and the worst she's shot is a Coke bottle."

Barker was still trying to feel them out. He didn't like the fact that they wanted the guns immediately. He had his radar out, Julia could sense it. But there was one thing about radar, it didn't tell you a thing if you didn't give it a target. Julia closed the discussion.

"We'll take two," she said. "Along with two boxes of shells."

Barker gave them buckshot—triple lot, he called it, very heavy steel pellets. Barker warned them that if they hit someone at close range, they'd blow them wide open. Julia quickly picked out a new jacket for Jim. It was big and warm and completely snow-white. Jim paid for the stuff with a credit card.

The mall was only an hour from the liquor store on Barnes. Jim drove straight toward it at high speed. Julia wanted to get there early, in case Frank and his buddy decided to pull the job before eleven. She wondered what Amy was doing that very moment and how she had found out Frank's name. But most of all she wondered if Scott was still alive. She felt that he must be. If he'd died, she believed his ghost would come to her, come to say goodbye.

Of course, her mother had not come to her.

As they approached the lake near the liquor store, Julia gazed out the window at the moon reflecting on the water. The moonlight affected Julia deeply. It seemed to condense her sense of time into a tight ball, from which she was able to experience everything that had happened in the past twenty-four hours as if it were all happening now, in the present.

She relived the experience of riding in the car with her friends, the dizziness when she rubbed Jim's sore neck, the horror of Scott's shooting, the hatred of the kid who had done the shooting, the agony of waiting for Scott's operation to finish, the comfort of Jim's companionship, the anxiety of her aunt's pursuit. She experienced all these things outside a logical sequence. The experiences were all one, not separate from one another. They were interwoven like the threads of a tapestry. Yet there was a core idea to the experiences, around which all the others formed. It was her hatred for Frank. Since she first glimpsed him in the pond, she had hated him with a feeling so strong it seemed to have a life of its own.

I dreamed of a bloody lagoon with a monster lurking in the depths. I sent Scott down under to deal with it. I sent Scott into the gas station to his death. I sent him to Frank. But I did not see Frank in the lagoon. I was alone with the monster in the end.

The reflection of moonlight on the water turned to blood. Julia tried to shake herself from her vision. She tapped Jim's shoulder. "Do you see that?" she whispered.

He glanced over and paled. "It's red."

She turned to him. "You can see it?"

He nodded.

"You have to get away from me."

"I can't," Jim said.

"Why not?"

"I love you," he stated simply.

"That's not good."

"It's not bad. Why don't we go somewhere else tonight?"

It was her turn. "I can't. I have too much hate."

Mom said love is stronger than hate. He may be stronger than me.

Julia prayed that Jim could save them both.

Chapter
Twelve

THE Truckwater house sat reflected in the high beams like a nightmare. The driveway was a pile of loose asphalt, and the front porch was ready to be used for firewood. Paint peeled from the clapboards like diseased skin. There was no light anyplace. Amy had driven far to reach her destination, but as she sat in her car and stared at the dark and forbidding place, she prayed there was no one home. If Frank Truckwater lived inside, she thought, he had to be rotten like the building.

Amy got out of her car and walked toward the front door, twice stumbling on the weed-choked lawn. The doorbell hung loose and impotent from its rusty socket, like an eye that had been gouged from an animal. Amy knocked hesitantly and listened for the sound of moving feet, the cocking of a revolver. It was only then she realized that she must have been half mad to pay a visit in the dark to a possible murderer. No sound came from inside.

Amy tried the door. It was locked.

"Hello?" she called.

Still no sound.

Amy circled around back. The house was small, and if time and nature had their way, it would be gone soon. The elements had labored long on its supporting beams, and it looked ready to collapse. Amy stepped to the back door. It, too, was locked, but when she pounded on the door it suddenly swung open.

Yes, Amy, come inside. I'll give you a red ribbon to wear around your head, too. How is your friend? Was my ribbon too tight?

Amy stepped through the door. The night was cold, but the house was colder. A foul odor touched her nose, a smell that only rats would cherish. She tried the light switch by the door, without luck. She had a small flashlight in her purse. Taking it out and turning it on, she scanned what had once been the kitchen but what was now a cesspool. It looked as if Frank had cooked a turkey dinner the previous Thanksgiving and left the leftovers in the sink and on the counter for ten months. Amy found it impossible to imagine that anyone could live in the place.

Amy explored deeper into the house, through the living room and then into the two bedrooms. There was no furniture in any of the rooms. In the smaller of the two bedrooms a mat and a sleeping bag lay on the floor beside a pile of unwashed clothes. The aroma of marijuana was heavy and sweet, almost covering another mysterious odor she couldn't identify. Amy knew very little about drugs. She had been drunk only once in her life, and that had been at her parents' Christmas Eve party. It had been fun while it lasted, but she had awoken the next morning with a headache so severe it had been difficult to open her presents.

130

On the wall at the head of the mat a picture of a guy and a girl sitting on a motorcycle was pinned. Their arms were wrapped around each other, wild grins on their sunburned faces. Amy removed the picture and studied it under the beam of her flashlight. The girl looked vaguely familiar, although it took Amy a moment to understand why.

She has Julia's eyes. Bright green. Beautiful. This is Kary Florence, Julia's half-sister.

It had been Kary Florence.

The guy wasn't so ugly as the one Julia had described to the police. In fact, he was kind of cute, in a sly sort of way. He didn't have a mustache, yet the more Amy stared at the picture, the more convinced she became that she was looking at the person who had sent Scott to the edge of death. The dark features and thin build were identical to Julia's description, and something else her friend had said to Lieutenant Crawley came back to haunt Amy.

"He has a vacantness about him. The lights are on, but nobody's home. He looks like one of those guys that evil works through. Like a Charles Manson or an Adolf Hitler. He appears more a vehicle of something, than a person."

Lieutenant Crawley had not been impressed by Julia's insight, wanting less imagery and more details. Focusing harder on Frank Truckwater's face, trying to see beneath his superficial handsomeness, Amy felt cold. She had to remind herself that this was the preaccident Frank Truckwater, the one with a cute girlfriend riding on the back of his bike. It didn't help. He may have been happier before Kary's accident, but he had still been heading for a bad end.

At the wrong end of a smoking gun.

Amy spotted an empty box of bullets on the floor beneath the window. Picking it up, she knew it wasn't conclusive proof. The box wouldn't stand up in court. She didn't even know the caliber of the bullet that had torn into Scott's head, if it matched that listed on the side of the box. Yet, for Amy, all her doubts were dispelled in that instant.

Frank Truckwater was the one who had shot Scott Hague.

And Julia is on to him. And she's got my boyfriend with her.

Amy realized, for all the separate threads she had tied together, she had nothing to take to the police. Indeed, her entire investigation of Frank had been based on a passing comment by Julia's aunt. Crawley would not be impressed, she knew, by the fact that the woman had mysterious *powers.*

Who are those women? What *are they?*

What was Julia?

On the phone Jim had given Amy the impression that he and Julia were pressed for time. That could only mean that Julia expected to confront Frank soon. But where? At another holdup? Amy went through the rest of the house. She found nothing more, except a disconnected phone. She was on the verge of leaving when she decided to check the garage.

It wasn't nearly so disgusting as the house, which wasn't to say it was neat. But at least the tools were in order on the workbench, and even if there were oil stains everywhere, the stains didn't stink. Amy suspected that Frank spent more time in the garage than in the house.

She didn't look long before she found two noteworthy articles. The first was a clear glass tube with a hollow ball at one end, a fluted mouthpiece at the other. At the top of the ball was a small hole; at the bottom, a dark lump of melted crystal. The ball was scorched black; it had obviously been held above a flame. She sniffed the open end of the tube.

Vanilla?

It was not vanilla, but the odor was similar. Amy couldn't identify the drug, but she knew Frank was smoking something that wasn't good for him. The tube was stained on the outside with what looked like transmission fluid—it felt warm.

He probably left just before I got here.

The second thing Amy found was a little black book. It was filled with neatly printed names, phone numbers, addresses, plus carefully listed amounts. For example: "Robert Rutherford 2 grams $35 > $40." Amy figured Robert had bought two grams of whatever Frank was selling for thirty-five dollars a gram, and that he still owed forty bucks. It didn't surprise her that Frank was a dealer.

At the back of the book was a separate list of names. They were of gas stations, liquor stores, convenience stores, small markets. Amy almost jumped out of her skin when she saw the gas station where Scott had been shot listed. Beside the name and address, Frank had jotted down a number of details about each place. With the gas station he had written: "old man on duty, back door, easy lock, open till twelve, attached food, no alarm, probably no gun." It appeared Frank never hit a place without scoping it out first.

There were literally three dozen places listed, some as far away as fifty miles. Amy had no idea how to begin figuring out where he would hit next, but a reddish smudge beside a liquor store caught her eye.

Amy rubbed the stain between her fingertips, then used the fingers on her other hand to test the transmission fluid on the glass tube. They felt exactly the same.

He smoked his drugs, then just before he left he consulted his little black book for the details. "1645 Barnes Road. Closes at eleven. Cage in the back. Strong lock. Alarm. Maybe gun. Middle-aged man. Owner. Safe in the back. Good business."

Amy checked her watch. It was ten-thirty. The liquor store was about twenty miles away. Frank would probably try hitting it as near to closing as possible—when business would be at its slowest. Amy gathered the glass tube and the black book together. She was turning to leave when she bumped into someone.

"Ah!" she screamed.

She dropped her light, and it went off. Pitch blackness fell over her, along with two powerful hands.

"Did I scare you, Amy?"

It took her a moment to realize it was Randy Classick, but her relief in that instant was outweighed by her fury. She shook off his hands.

"Don't you ever sneak up on me like that!" she said. "I could have peed in my pants." Amy dropped to her knees and searched for her flashlight. It was not broken, and when she turned it on, Randy was grinning from ear to ear.

"Are you sure you didn't pee in them?" he asked.

"No. Yes! You're smelling the drugs this guy smokes. Here, look at this." She handed him the glass tube. Randy took a whiff of it and winced.

"Heavy stuff," he said.

"What is it?"

"Crystal meth. Speed."

"Is it dangerous?" she asked.

"Speed kills."

"Have you ever used it?"

"Once. It was enough. It's more addicting than crack."

Amy opened the black book to the Barnes Road liquor-store entry. She pointed out the smudge on the tube and beside the entry, and she told him her conclusions. Randy was impressed by her detective work. He agreed that they should drive to the liquor store at warp speed. But he wanted to call the cops first.

"The phone inside the house doesn't work," she said.

"We'll find one on the way there," he said, heading for the door. "We better take your car. I'm out of gas."

"Did you follow the aunt and her group?"

"Yeah."

"Where are they?"

"Probably at the gas station," Randy said, pleased with himself.

"Huh?"

"I'll explain in the car."

"How did you know I'd be here?"

"You said you were going to the Florences' and then the Truckwaters'. I figured you'd be here by now. I hope we get this guy. You know, I'm missing a late dinner with that waitress he introduced me to last night. I'm supposed to be at Sally's house right now."

"Good old Sally. Did you tell her what happened to Scott?"

"Yeah. She was going to bring him by a pie from her diner."

"Didn't you tell her he's in a coma?"

"Nah," Randy said. "I didn't want to depress her. You can't undress a woman who's depressed."

"You're a pervert, did I ever tell you that?"

"The world's full of them."

Chapter Thirteen

JULIA and Jim knelt behind a group of trees with their shotguns ready. They had left Scott's car a quarter of a mile down the road, hidden in a thicket. The lake was off to their right, the moon bright on its cold surface, the liquor store fifty yards in front of them, empty except for the man behind the counter, waiting to close. The time was exactly ten forty-two. They had been waiting for ten minutes.

"I just had an idea," Jim whispered.

"What?"

"Let's go in and warn the man that he's about to be held up."

"I never thought of that," Julia said, surprised by her own lack of foresight. "Do you think he'd believe us?"

"Maybe. Maybe not. But he would probably close the store a few minutes early."

"I don't want him to close the store," Julia said.

"Why not?"

"The guys will come and then drive on. They'll get away."

"That's true," Jim said. "But we might save the man inside from getting shot."

Julia had never thought of that, either. Jim was right. She felt a stab of guilt at her next words. "But when will we have another chance like this?" she asked.

It was dark—she couldn't see Jim's expression. Yet something in his voice made her wonder if he believed they were sitting in the dark and cold for nothing.

"There will always be another chance," he said.

"Maybe," Julia said, thoughtful.

What am I more afraid of? That the man inside the store will die? Or that Frank and his partner have changed their minds and are not coming? If they don't come, Jim will think I'm a fool.

Julia realized that for someone who didn't want people to know she had powers, she sure didn't want to be known for *not* having them either. She was a hypocrite, pure and simple. If she hadn't been showing off her supergirl massage fingers to Jim in the first place, Scott wouldn't have got shot.

"What's that?" Jim asked, sitting up, suddenly alert. The roar was far off, maybe as much as two miles. But there was no mistaking what it was.

"Motorcycles," Julia whispered.

"Right," Jim said.

Now they were too late to warn the man inside the store. The bikes must have been doing ninety miles an hour. They roared into sight in little over a minute. Julia found herself holding her breath as she caught sight of Frank—the guy in the mustache, the guy who put her friend in the hospital, the guy who cursed her

138

mother, the guy who was going to pay. It was only then that Julia thought what she had known she was going to do all along—she would kill him.

Frank and his friend circled the liquor store once before parking in the front. Julia and Jim had also taken a quick look around the place. Julia remembered the fenced-in cage at the back of the store that was used for storage. It had a door but was locked tight at the moment, an important piece of information. There was only one way in, one way out. Frank and his pal could easily be cornered.

"Is that them?" Jim whispered.

"Oh, yes."

"Maybe we should rush them now, before they have a chance to go inside."

Julia shook her head. "They'd see us coming, and the guy with the mustache is quick with his gun." She squinted through the trees at the guys as they got off their bikes and walked toward the front door, their hands stuffed in the pockets of their leather jackets. The short fat kid moved with noticeable difficulty, his shoulders slouched over. Julia raised her shotgun and aimed along the barrel. "I suppose they're too far away to hit from here," she whispered.

Jim chuckled nervously. "We couldn't shoot them in cold blood."

Julia fingered the trigger. "Yeah."

The two disappeared inside. Julia and Jim let half a minute go by. Jim began to fidget. "What are we waiting for?" he asked.

"They'll relax just as they're about to finish the job."

"We won't know when that is. It could be now."

"I'll know," Julia said, her eyes glued to the store.

From their angle, unfortunately, they could see little more than the front door. They had yet to hear a sound, a cry for help, anything.

"But they might kill the man," Jim protested.

"If they were going to kill him, he'd be dead already, and we would have heard the shot. Be patient."

Julia let another two minutes go by, while the tension grew. Yet she knew she was sensing the confidence of those inside. It was late. The road was deserted. They could work at their leisure, they thought, and make sure they didn't miss anything.

Then a jolt went through the length of Julia's body, powerful as an electric shock. It seemed to strike at her from the direction of the lake. When she turned to see the moonlight on the water, it was white now, not red, white as Jim's new jacket. The color gave her no comfort. White held all the colors of the rainbow, she remembered, and when seen in a prism it could be as red as it was green. She wondered if that was why the future could only be glimpsed in the light of the moon, a future of all possibilities. Yet just as quickly she suspected what was wrong. There might only be one future, already set, and nothing she did would make one damn bit of difference. Julia glanced over at Jim and his new jacket.

"It's time," she said.

They stood, and Jim leapt out from behind the trees, anxious to get on with it. "Wait," Julia called softly. She lowered her gun and held out her arms. "Kiss me."

"Julia?"

"Now. Please?"

He kissed her and held her and told her again that

he loved her. It was a special kiss. It brought a gentle feeling of warmth to her chest. He was a special guy. She wanted to tell him that she loved him. But she couldn't. She was a witch, a bad witch. When he let go of her and turned toward the store, she quickly shifted the shotgun in her hands, holding it as if it were a baseball bat.

Forgive me.

Julia smacked Jim hard on the back of the skull with the butt of the shotgun. A choked sound of surprise passed his lips, and he fell to the ground. Julia glanced down at him as she stepped over his head. She did not pause to feel his head. His eyes were closed, his breathing even. She hoped she hadn't hit him too hard, and she hoped she'd hit him hard enough.

"Sleep, my sweet," she said. "I'll be back soon."

Julia pumped her shotgun and strode toward the liquor store.

She moved silently on her sneakers. She had always been adept at moving swiftly and quietly. In seconds she passed through the trees and crossed the parking lot. She felt the heat of the motorcycles' engines as she crept around them, crouched low. A glance through the front door showed her nothing, so she scurried right up beside the door, pressing close to a Seagram's 7 poster in the big picture window. Still, she didn't hear a peep from inside. For a moment she considered staying where she was and catching them as they came out the door. But guilt about the owner's well-being came back to haunt her. She was not omniscient. She could be sure of nothing. Perhaps Frank intended to kill the man, but not until the end of the holdup, when the man had told Frank where all the goodies were hidden.

Julia risked a peek around the poster.

The fat kid with the aching guts stood at the end of a long gray cashier's counter, near a narrow hallway that led to the rear of the store. He was leaning against the wall, holding a pistol instead of a shotgun this time. The store owner was nowhere to be seen, and the fat kid appeared to be distracted. He kept glancing into the hall behind him. Julia would have wagered money that Frank was in the back with the man, working on a safe maybe. The fat kid looked lousy, pale and shaken. Julia hoped she had given him a good case of internal bleeding.

She was about to give him another one.

Julia swung around the door and into the store, her shotgun ready at her shoulder. The fat kid was staring into the hall as she entered—she was halfway down the counter before he turned around. It was pathetic. He nearly fainted. He may as well have had a squirt gun in his hand for all the good it did him. He fumbled to bring the weapon up, but his arm appeared to be made of lead and his fingers plaster. He opened his mouth to shout for help, but the *Frank!* formed by his lips came out soundlessly. Julia locked the end of her barrel between his eyebrows and caressed the trigger.

For my friend, Scott, a face full of steel.

Yet the sheer devastation of the fellow betrayed Julia's desire for revenge. He couldn't have been more than sixteen, and no one knew better than she that he hadn't wanted to come along. Then again, he was no fan of hers. He wanted her dead as much as Frank. Plus if she didn't put him out of action, she wouldn't be able to get to Frank.

Julia lowered her shotgun below his waist.

"Frank," he finally managed to croak out. He raised his pistol higher.

She pulled her trigger first.

The fat kid's right knee exploded in a shower of red. *Gross. Sick. Yuck.*

He dropped to the floor. She had not blown off his leg, but close. He slumped against the wall and dropped his pistol. His eyes bulged from his head as he stared down at the horrible mess she had made of his body. Yet there wasn't much in the eyes. He was in shock. It was good, in a way. He didn't actually appear to be in pain. His blood dripped in a narrow stream onto the yellow linoleum floor, forming a puddle that widened toward a stack of Bud Light.

Julia crossed the floor and crouched beside the fat kid, glancing down the hall that led to the back. She saw nothing and pocketed the pistol. The weapon was small, silver, a miniature Colt six-shooter. It was then she noticed the owner of the store. Her guess had been wrong. He lay unconscious behind the counter, an ugly red wound on the back of his head. It looked as if Frank had done the same number on the owner as she had on Jim—but with a lot less love.

Her glance at the man pulled Julia's vision to the right, toward the front of the store. It was only for an instant, but as she turned back toward the hall, she caught sight of a figure out of the corner of her eye. She didn't wait to get a good look at him. She jerked back, and in that second the top of the long gray counter— exactly where her head had been—splintered in a jagged crater from a bullet.

Julia leapt to her feet and pressed her body against

the wall adjacent to the hallway. The fat kid on the floor let out a soft moan. His head fell to his chest. He was out cold. She paid him no heed. Counting two beats of her pounding heart, she pumped her shotgun and whipped around the corner of the hall and let loose a shot.

She missed, and it was a pity because she was so close. As she had rounded the corner, Frank was in the middle of the hall, creeping slowly toward the front, the gun in his hand held ready. She might have startled him, because he didn't fire a shot of his own. Yet he had the reflexes of a cat. Before the screaming steel pellets could reach him, he was gone. He had dived into a storage area off the hall that contained boxes of booze that reached almost to the ceiling. Her shot went all the way through to the metal cage outside, where a crate of innocent Pepsi bottles erupted in a shower of glass slivers.

I didn't even graze him.

Julia jumped back to safety, flattening herself next to the hallway, accidentally bumping the kid's head with the butt of her gun.

She pumped her shotgun again and called out, "You have a wounded man out here, Frank. What do you say I don't plaster his brains on the wall if you come out with your hands up and your gun in your teeth?"

Frank took a moment to respond. When he did, his voice was as incredulous as it was angry. "Who the hell are you?"

"Don't you recognize me? We met last night. You remember. You shot my friend in the head."

Frank took another moment. "How did you know we'd be here?"

144

Julia smiled. "I was at your house, Frank. I watched you smoke your ice. I listened to your plans. King told me where I could find you. He sent me to blow you away."

"King doesn't know we're here."

"He's outside in his car. Why don't you surrender, and maybe he won't be too hard on you."

Frank thought about that awhile. Julia listened closely for any sound of movement but detected none. She considered changing positions. There was a tiny office—it looked hardly big enough to turn around in—just down the hall a couple of feet on the right. From there she might be able to get off a clean shot.

"You're a liar, bitch," Frank said finally. "There isn't a girl alive King would trust to do his dirty business. I do remember you. You're the daughter of that witch who worked in the hospital."

"That's right. I am a witch, and I know all about you. I know how you cursed my mother."

"What do you want?" Frank asked, getting bored.

"A little conversation, that's all. What do you want?"

Frank didn't answer, and that worried Julia. She strained her ears, this time imagining she could hear faint steps creeping her way. She risked a glance around the corner and didn't see him. She didn't want to wait until he came to her. The office it would have to be.

Keep your head low, girl. Real low.

Julia pumped her shotgun, held her breath for five seconds, and then swung around the corner, crouched low. No shots sounded. She squeezed into the coffin-size office and pressed against its rear wall. From there she was able to peer into the storage area across the hall. It seemed to be about twenty feet across, but it was so jammed with rows of boxes that little more than narrow walkways were left to move around in. Still, there was no sign of Frank. She suspected he was behind some boxes. She doubted that he would have retreated to the back cage area. Even if he were able to shoot the lock off the back door, he would still have to circle around to the front to get his motorcycle. Once out in the parking lot, he would have made an easy target.

No, he's not stupid. He'll wait for me to make a mistake.

The office held a desk, if it could be called that; it was little more than a stand, where the owner obviously did his paperwork. The top was littered with receipts, bills, checks, and so on. The man smoked; there was an ashtray, crammed full with dirty cigarette butts. Beside it lay a clear plastic Bic lighter. It got Julia thinking.

I'm in a liquor store. Liquor burns. It burns real good.

Julia picked up the lighter and slipped it into her pocket. But a sound off to her left distracted her right then. She peered out the office again, this time toward the front door. Just what she needed now, she thought: a customer.

Jim! What a hard head you have.

It was Jim all right, his shotgun in hand. He didn't look like he could put up much of a fight. Julia supposed a crack on the head would ruin anyone's reflexes. Jim staggered around the store like a drunk craving a bottle.

"Julia?" he called.

She had to betray her new position; there was no helping it.

"I'm here," she said. "Stay back. Stay back from the hallway. Frank's in the back."

Jim heard her, but when his eyes fastened on the fat kid and the exploded knee and puddle of blood, his humanity got the better of him. He hurried to the kid's side, crouching down not far from where she had hid a minute ago. The fat kid's fallen head did not stir.

Jim set aside his shotgun and felt the kid's pulse. "Julia, he's bleeding to death."

"Let him bleed!" Julia hissed. "I told you, Frank's in the back. You see that hole in the counter? That was supposed to be my brains."

A glance at the splintered counter sobered Jim somewhat. He picked up his shotgun. "We need an ambulance," he said.

"Later," she swore, peeking once more into the storage room. Frank had patience; she had to grant him that. There was still no sign of him. Perhaps knowing she had a backup had him worried. Yet Julia didn't think he would surrender.

He must know I want him dead.

Jim pressed into the corner adjacent to the hallway. He was four feet off to Julia's left, eight feet behind her. "Have you tried talking to him?" he whispered.

"Yes," she whispered back. "He's not very nice."

"Why did you hit me on the head?"

"I'm not very nice."

"Where's the owner?"

Julia gestured over her shoulder, back behind the counter. That was a mistake. Jim immediately felt it was his responsibility to examine the fellow. He jumped right across the opening of the hallway, causing Julia to suck in her breath. But Frank didn't shoot.

He's saving his bullets. Maybe he didn't bring extra ammo.

Julia's view of the space behind the counter was partially blocked. She could scarcely see Jim as he checked the owner. Even a glimpse at them required her to stick her head partway into the hallway. She cursed herself for not having hit Jim harder on the back of the skull. His companionship was doing nothing to improve her confidence. She wanted to scream that they could take care of the wounded later!

Julia pulled the lighter from her pocket and flicked it a couple of times to make sure it worked. A Molotov cocktail could be just the thing to bring Frank into the open. Jim might be of some help to her, after all. If he could get her a vodka bottle from behind the counter and a piece of cloth . . .

Julia poked her head out of the tiny office far enough to see Jim. With relief, she saw he had finished examining the owner and was crouched low and moving back in her direction, still behind the counter, relatively protected from a shot out of the storage area. She was about to call to Jim when she noticed the owner stir at his back. Whatever Jim had done had woken the guy up. Julia didn't know if that was good or bad.

A second later she decided it was definitely very bad.

The ability to see in slow motion that supposedly hit at moments of crisis didn't happen for Julia. Yet she did register everything that followed in exceptional clarity and detail.

The man stirred and opened his eyes. No doubt the first thing he saw was Jim, who had never seemed even vaguely threatening to Julia. If anything, he had a shy, innocent manner. On the other hand, he was big and muscular, and even if he was crawling away from the guy, he did have a shotgun in his hand. Julia could practically read the owner's thought. The guy had just been held up, banged in the head. He had to be groggy. How was he to know the good guys from the bad guys?

Julia watched in horror as the owner of the liquor store reached inside an empty cigar box hidden beneath a pile of brown paper bags and pulled out an automatic pistol.

"Jim!" she screamed. "Behind you! He's got a gun!"

Jim stood and whirled. The moment he was up, he became a target for Frank. Julia realized that instinctively, even before the pale hand with the black gun poked out from behind a row of boxes in the storage area. She realized something else then, too. Frank didn't have to show his head to fire. He had a crack between the pile of boxes that gave him a clear view. There was no way else to explain how he had the point of his gun lined up so perfectly between Jim's shoulder blades.

Julia had to make a decision, and she had to make it quick. She had to decide who stood the better chance of killing Jim. The owner was much closer to him. His aim was unobstructed. Frank was thirty feet back and was peering around piles of boxes. Yet the owner was still dazed. He scarcely had a hold on his weapon. Frank could squeeze his trigger any second, and Julia knew from experience that he was a good shot.

He hit Scott clean enough.

Julia leapt into the middle of the hallway, putting

herself between Frank's gun and Jim's back. Once more she might have startled Frank. His gun wavered slightly. Julia fired a shot directly at it.

A bright orange spark exploded where her target had been.

Then there was nothing there.

I hit him! Did I hit him?

Julia quickly pumped her shotgun and let loose a blast into the box around which Frank's pistol had pointed. Bottles splattered, and dark liquid poured out. She pumped again and fired again.

Julia jumped back to her previous position, behind the corner next to the hallway, next to the fat kid, who was still unconscious. She whirled around just in time to watch Jim stare incredulously as the owner of the store steadied his shaking arm on a toppled wastebasket and aimed his gun. The owner was still flat on the floor, still bleeding, but he had fight left in him, even if he was confused about who his tormentors were.

Move! Move!

It was a night of bullets, of blood, Julia thought. But Jim couldn't comprehend what was happening. He could not free himself of the misperception of his innocence. He didn't really believe he could be punished. He did not understand that he committed the worst of all evils when he had stayed in the car and Scott went into the convenience store. But Julia understood. He had cheated destiny once—he wouldn't cheat her a second time.

Julia dived at Jim just as she had dived at Scott. She flew through the air with her eyes wide open. She was the same millisecond too late. The owner of the store fired his gun. A spot of red appeared in the center of

Jim's jacket. Julia crashed into him, and together they hit the floor. Quickly she rolled Jim over, telling herself she hadn't heard the shot, that there would be nothing to see. Unfortunately the spot of red was still there. She put her hand over it, pressing down on his chest wound, as if it were some small cut that would respond to mild pressure, but it swelled rapidly. It was incredible how it swelled. In seconds the entire front of his jacket was soaked with blood. Yeah, that was right, now he was wearing his red jacket.

Julia glanced back at the owner. He had his gun pointed at her now. But he was having problems of his own. He trembled like a man coming off a fix. Julia gave him one hard look and he fainted.

Because she was on the floor beside her fallen partner, Julia had the counter for protection from Frank's sniper fire. She couldn't stay where she was, however. She had dropped her shotgun when she had dived at Jim. It lay flat across the opening to the hallway. Of course, she did have Jim's shotgun at her disposal. It had all five shells left in its chamber. It was primed and ready, but Julia couldn't take Jim's gun from him. It would be like taking the sword from the fallen gladiator. She'd have to admit to herself that Jim was dead.

He can't be alive, Julia. No one bleeds like that and stays alive for more than a couple of seconds, not from the chest.

Jim lay flat on his back, his eyes closed. He was not breathing. He did not make any sound when she shook him. He had on a red jacket, and her vision had implied that the color was important, one of the vital ingredients. Well, it was complete now, and no one knew better than Julia that visions never lied. It was decided. There was no need for a doctor's examination. Jim was dead.

Julia leaned over and kissed him on the lips.

"I love you, too," she said, knowing how late she was with the words.

She sat up and pulled off Jim's right shoe. She'd had enough of this waiting. It was time for some payback, a hell-flaming funeral pyre of payback. She yanked off Jim's sock and grabbed a fifth of one hundred and twenty proof tequila off the shelf at her back. Julia popped the top and poured a generous gulp over Jim's sock. Then she stuffed the sock into the neck of the bottle and got up.

There was no sign of Frank. Julia was thankful for small favors. She crawled over and retrieved her own shotgun and tried to remember how many times she had fired. Was it three or four times? She played it safe. She set down her Molotov cocktail and quickly reloaded. The weapon took five shells. She couldn't believe she had fired so many times. She glanced at the unconscious kid. Jim was right: he needed an ambulance and soon. Julia felt nothing for him. She felt nothing, period. She was a void. She had only one purpose, and that was to destroy Frank.

Julia decided to return to the tiny office before tossing her firebomb. The position would bring her closer to the storage area and would also give her a better angle on Frank when he fled the flames. Pumping her shotgun, Julia again spun around the corner and leapt into the claustrophobic space. Again, Frank left her alone, and she found that odd.

There was a spark. Did I hit his gun?

Julia wasted no time debating the issue. Balancing

her shotgun in one hand and the Molotov cocktail in the other, she managed to wiggle the lighter from her pocket. She flicked on the flame and touched it to the rag. The fire caught quickly. In fact, it caught so quickly that she feared the stupid thing would explode in her hand. Rather than setting down her gun and throwing it hard as she planned, she hastily tossed it toward the storage area. The mistake was hers alone, and she cursed her stupidity. She hadn't put enough arc into the throw. The bottle bounced on the concrete floor and failed to crack open and explode.

They always blow up in the movies.

The bottle sat on the floor and leisurely burned away at Jim's white sock. Julia supposed she could wait for it to finish with its fuse, but she was tired of waiting. She had been waiting since she'd looked in the pond in the moonlight. Stepping directly into the hallway, she lowered her shotgun and fired.

The bottle blew up. The tequila splattered the boxes of booze, and suddenly there was fire everywhere. At the same instant, a bullet whizzed by her head and ripped off a crystal earring Amy had given her, along with a piece of her ear.

He's above me!

Frank was on top of the boxes, flat on his belly only a couple of feet beneath the ceiling. He must have climbed up while the owner was killing Jim. Julia saw him only as a squirming shadow through a crackling orange glow. Instinctively she pressed against the hallway wall across from the tiny office. Another bullet whizzed by, taking out a chunk of brown paneling. She had reacted correctly, but now what the hell was she supposed to do? Blood streamed down the right side of her neck out of a mushy area of pain.

Her ear was bleeding, and her earring was ruined. It made no sense why that latter fact bothered her so much, but suddenly she didn't care—about anything, not even her own life. She just wanted to get Frank. Pumping her shotgun, she jumped *toward* the storage area, hugging the wall.

"Die!" she screamed, whirling into the open for a shot. "Die!"

Julia fired twice and had no idea what she hit, except that it was probably cases full of flammable alcohol. Glass flew and booze spurted as the fire roared higher and higher. The devil himself could have breathed on the flames. Every inch of her exposed flesh screamed at her that she was really back in the boiling lagoon, with the monster from below blowing smoke bubbles all around. Only this monster was coming from above, coming fast. Before Julia could pump her shotgun for a third shot, the squirming shadow suddenly leapt down upon her.

Frank's chest hit her squarely in the face. It was not a controlled leap on his part by any means. He hit the concrete floor as hard as she did, which Julia knew was pretty hard. They fell apart, lying side by side on the floor. Pain flared through the back of her skull. She fought back a gray film that threatened to descend over her eyes. She knew that if she blacked out, she was dead. Rolling her head to the side, she watched as he twice tried to raise himself up from his prone position and failed. She noticed one of his problems: he was missing a hunk of his right shoulder. One of her blasts had hit him. He also seemed to have misplaced his gun in the fall. She was relieved about that, until she saw him reach into his pocket and pull out a slim silver object. A faint click followed, and then the orange light of the fire gleamed at the tip of a long, shiny razor.

A switchblade!

Julia immediately regained her wits. She got onto her knees. Her shotgun lay between her and Frank. He was getting up slowly, in staggering jerks. Excitement burst in Julia's chest. One shot and he'd be history. Reaching down, she grabbed the stock of the gun and began to bring it up. But Frank was either not as hurt as he appeared, or else he died hard. With his free hand he slammed the barrel down to the floor just as Julia got her finger around the trigger. The gun went off, sending a useless blast into the wall. Wood splinters sprayed around them both. Because Julia did not have a solid grip on the shotgun, the recoil was fierce. The barrel spun around and struck her square in the jaw. Julia saw stars, galaxies even, whirling in crazy patterns, with a long silver spaceship in the center that looked vaguely familiar. Too late she realized that it was Frank's knife moving toward her neck.

"Don't move," he whispered as he pressed the blade to her throat with his left hand. He was a mess. His right hand couldn't have had a square inch of firm flesh left on the back of it. She must have hit it when she saw the orange spark. That meant the shots he had fired at her after that had been with his left hand. It was probably the only reason she was still alive. She was one lucky girl. Right. He pressed the blade deeper into her skin, close to cutting depth. His eyes, although filled with fury, nevertheless struck her as oddly blank.

He's smoked too much ice.

There was another kind of smoke in the air. Bottle after bottle of liquor blew up behind them, choking the hallway with thick, black fumes. Julia could feel the heat of the fire prickling the skin of her face. She coughed, trying not to move. Yet she felt strangely unafraid. Perhaps it was because she was still bursting with anger. If she had a knife at his throat, she wouldn't have hesitated. She would have slit his arteries wide open. He gestured for her to stand.

"Slowly," he cautioned.

Julia slid up with her back against the wall. Frank kept the tip of his blade close to her throat the whole time, although he had more difficulty standing than she had. His right shoulder had to be hurting. It was hard to tell where his shredded leather jacket left off and his wound began. Sweat dripped from the end of his greasy mustache.

"What's your name?" he asked.

"Julia Florence."

The name startled him. "What's your last name?"

"Florence."

He stared at her eyes a moment, then shook his head faintly. "How do you know my name? How did you know we'd be here tonight?"

"If I told you, you wouldn't believe me."

"Try me."

"Go to hell."

He grinned. "You're frisky."

Just then Julia remember the fat kid's small pistol in her coat pocket. She also remembered the other weapon she held in her secret pocket, in her head. There had been too much excitement since she had entered the store to retry her mental knife. At the moment, however, the circumstances couldn't have been more perfect. It had worked the first time when her fury was at its peak. If fury was what fueled it, she

156

had a full tank right then. She looked down at his injured shoulder, concentrating on making it fall apart.

Pain, Frank. I want you to hurt like I hurt. I want you to hurt worse.

An intangible force seemed to move between them right then. It was not visible, yet the smoke that rose about them suddenly parted, as if a huge hand had been thrust through from another dimension. Julia sensed the power of it, but she felt no ability to control it. In fact, she wasn't even sure if it was really there, if it wasn't just a product of her imagination. Nevertheless, it scared her, worse than Frank's knife. She wasn't sure if *it* knew who it was supposed to attack.

"Die, Frank," she whispered, trying to give *it* direction. "Die."

Frank jerked back involuntarily, pulling the knife from her throat. Julia couldn't be sure if he had reacted to her suggestion, or if an injured nerve brought about his spasm. It did seem that while she felt the *power* between them, the blood flow from his shoulder dramatically increased. In either case, the spasm was enough to give her a chance to reach in her pocket and pull out the pistol. Before Frank could recover, she had rammed the nozzle into the base of his chin. The intangible force between them dissolved. She may have felt she could bring it back at a moment's notice, but there was nothing like a good solid gun to finish off a prolonged fight.

"Drop it," she said softly.

Frank surveyed the situation, thought about it for a second, and then dropped his switchblade. He started to back up a step. She shook her head.

"Stay," she said.

He was not grinning now. "I should have hit you last night."

She almost spat in his face. "Like you hit Scott."

"He got in my way."

"Yeah? Well, you're in my way now."

He was unimpressed. "What are you going to do, kill me?"

She smiled. "That's right."

He snorted. "You're just like your mother."

Julia lost her smile. "Why did you curse my mother?"

He regarded her for a moment, and that something that had seemed to be missing from his eyes flashed briefly. It confused Julia. But a flash in the dark wasn't the same as a sunrise. Frank hardened once more.

"Go to hell," he said, repeating her line of a second ago.

You go first and tell me how the weather is.

Julia felt justified. She tightened her grip on the trigger.

Then she heard a noise. A very loud noise.

Chapter Fourteen

AMY and Randy found a pay phone halfway between Frank's place and the liquor store. They called the police and were patched directly into Lieutenant Crawley. Amy told him she had a hot lead on Scott's shooting, and he sounded suspicious.

"Where are you calling from?" he asked, as if that mattered in the slightest.

"I don't know," she said. "A phone booth somewhere. Look, those guys who shot my friend are going to hit a liquor store on Barnes, the one by the lake."

"How do you know?" Crawley asked.

"I was just at Frank Truckwater's house. He's one of the hoods."

"And he told you he was going to rob this liquor store tonight?"

"No! He wasn't there. But I saw his notes on the place. He's a drug dealer and a thief. You've got to believe me. Get someone out there immediately."

"What did you say your name was?"

"Amy Belle."

159

"You're Julia Florence's friend, aren't you?"

"Yes."

There was a long pause. "Are you feeding me a line?"

"No."

"Does Julia have anything to do with your calling?"

"I think Julia's at the liquor store right now."

Amy deliberately phrased the remark to give Crawley the impression that Julia might be in on the holdup. Why Julia's best friend would be calling to report her probably didn't cross his mind. Julia was right—Crawley was dumb.

"Where did you say the liquor store is?" Crawley asked.

"On Barnes, by the lake. Are you going to send out a car?"

"I'm going myself."

"Good." Amy hung up the phone and jogged back to the idling car, yelling at Randy, "Let's go!"

Amy knew Randy was not the best of drivers under ordinary circumstances. On their one and only date he had accidentally run over a dog. But he was behind the wheel now, for better or worse, and he was pushing her car for all it was worth. They flew along a narrow road lined with pines, seemingly chasing their own headlights. Randy kept letting the car wander over the dividing line.

"Careful," she said.

"You're telling me to be careful and we're rushing to a holdup without a gun?" he remarked, bringing the car back in line.

"I never thought of that." She checked her watch: six minutes to eleven. "We don't have time to stop to get one."

"We're going to get there before the cops. If this Frank guy is there, what are we going to do, scare him into a citizen's arrest with our angry voices?"

"I tell you, we don't have time."

"All right. But let's plan a bit.

"OK. What should we do?"

"Let's ram the store."

"This isn't a stupid football game," Amy said, annoyed. "You're not ramming anything with my car."

She had hurt his feelings. "You really think football's stupid?"

"Yes."

"Is that why you only went out with me once, 'cause I'm on the team?" Randy asked.

"No."

"What was the reason, then?"

"I can't believe you're asking a question like this at a time like this."

"I was just trying to make conversation." Randy concentrated on his driving for a couple of minutes. They were doing over ninety. Then he spoke again. "Am I too poor?"

"Randy, really, it's not the time."

"But I might get shot in a few minutes. I might die."

"You're not going to die, for Christsake."

"Aren't I handsome enough for you?" he asked.

"No, that wasn't it."

"What was it, then?"

Amy looked over at him. "You're crude and disgusting."

He wasn't insulted. "That's all?"

"That's a lot."

Randy shrugged. "It's nothing permanent. I can act

civilized when I have to." He paused. "If I'm real nice to you for a whole month, and don't do anything disgusting, would you go out with me?"

"Randy, why do you want to go out with me? I'm not that cute. What's so special about me?"

"I figure you'll be easy to get in the sack."

Amy would have punched him if he hadn't begun to creep over the line again. Instead she laughed. "Let me think about it," she told him.

Amy was not laughing when they caught sight of the liquor store a few minutes later. Smoke was pouring out the front. The back was aglow with flickering orange light.

"Something's happening," Randy said grimly.

"Pull in beside the store," Amy said. "Cut the engine when you hit the parking lot. Don't make any noise stopping."

"All right. But I'm going in first."

"Don't be too eager to act the hero, or you might not be going out with anybody."

Randy hit a trash can, bringing the car to a halt. It was filled with glass bottles and aluminum beer cans, and if they had set off fireworks, they couldn't have announced their arrival better. Amy swore at him and jumped out of the car. She scurried around to the front, keeping her head low. Randy was slow in catching up. A glance over the booze posters in the windows showed her nothing but black smoke. She moved to the door and risked sticking her head inside.

The first thing she saw was the fire raging in the back. It was a monster, and she knew the store was lost, even if a fire engine showed up in the next minute. There appeared to be two figures standing in front of the fire, but it was impossible to tell who they were or what they were doing. The smaller of the two glanced her way before suddenly backing into the rear of the store, disappearing into the smoke and flames. Then Amy caught sight of the fat kid lying on the floor against the wall, and her stomach heaved.

His right leg was hamburger, and his head had fallen and he was drooling on his chest. Amy recognized him because of Julia's description. There was a puddle of blood around him big enough to feed a flock of vampire bats. Even before Amy entered the store, she knew it had to have been Julia who shot him.

She had time to stop and arm herself.

Still crouching low, Amy swept in past the counter toward the fallen kid. Besides wanting to keep out of sight, she stayed down to keep from choking; the majority of the smoke was in the upper half of the store. Reaching the kid, she knelt by his side and checked his pulse, all the time straining to see who was in the back. Whoever they were, they must be mad. She could hardly breathe where she was.

I'll have to go back there, though. It's got to be Julia and Frank.

The fat kid's heart was racing thin and weak. Amy was considering what to fashion a tourniquet with to stop his bleeding when she spotted Jim on the floor behind the counter. He had on his red jacket, she thought, the one Julia didn't like. Only this one looked a little different.

A little wet.

"Oh, God," Amy whispered, forgetting the fat kid, the fire, the people in the back. She hurried to his side. There was a hole in his chest, and as Amy put her hand over it she couldn't help but notice how deep it was. She feared it went all the way into his heart. His face was white. She shook him gently.

"Jim?"

He opened his eyes. "Amy?"

"Yes!" she cried, a burst of relief melting her heart. She pressed her face close to his. "I'm here. I'm right here. You're going to be fine."

He continued to stare straight up, his blue eyes flat and unblinking. "I can't see you. I can't see anything."

"That's OK, that doesn't matter." She took his hand in hers. "I'm going to call an ambulance right now. We're going to get you a doctor."

Anxiety creased his features. "I'm cold, Amy. There's something wrong with me. I don't feel right."

Amy stroked his hair. She remembered the day she met him, how much she had wanted to run her fingers through it. But now her fingers were covered with blood and she was only messing it up. Her relief flared and died. A tear slipped over her cheek. His skin was cold as ice. The doctor was going to be too late.

"You'll feel fine soon," she lied to him.

"What's wrong with me?"

"You've been hurt. It's nothing."

"Where's Julia? Is she all right?"

"She's fine."

"Where is she? The guy has a gun."

"Shh. The police have the guy. Everything's fine now. Just relax. Close your eyes. Rest. That's it."

Jim shut his eyes. He swallowed thickly, and a tremor went through the length of his body. Then he seemed to relax somewhat, although his breathing remained difficult.

"I thought you would come," he said.

She smiled, and her tears flowed freely now. "Of course I came. I knew you'd be here."

"You're not mad at me for running off with Julia?"

"No. I could never be mad at you. You're the best boyfriend a girl ever had."

His right cheek twitched. He looked worried. "I have to tell you something, Amy."

"No. You don't have to say anything."

"But I have to, Amy." He trembled once more. "I have to."

Amy pressed her mouth close to his ear. "I know you love her, Jim. I love her, too. That's fine. Love is good. You were always good to me." Her voice choked. "And I will always love you."

"You're a neat girl." Jim smiled faintly. "I guess I won't be playing in next week's game."

Those were his last words. A sudden violent shudder lifted his body a couple of inches off the floor, and then he went completely still. Amy buried her face in his chest. His blood was warm, even if he was already growing cold.

I'll go to that game, Jim. I'll sit in the stands. I'll watch you play, and it won't matter that I'm the only one who can see you. I'll know you're there. I'll just know.

"Amy," Randy said behind her, his hand on her shoulder, his voice kind and concerned. "You can't stay with Jim. You have to get out of here. That guy's still here."

She raised her head, feeling weak, and wiped at her red face. "Where's Julia?"

"She's with Frank in the back."

"Is he holding her hostage?"

Randy had a shotgun in his hand. Amy vaguely

recalled one lying beside Jim. For the first time, Amy noticed the liquor-store manager unconscious on the floor behind his cash register. He didn't look so hot, either. He was coughing in his sleep.

"I think it's the other way around," Randy said. "I called out to them, and Julia shouted for me to butt out."

"Are you sure she said that?"

"Yeah."

Amy got up. "Stay here with my boyfriend."

Randy put a hand out to stop her. "There's no way you're going back there. You'll suffocate, if you don't burn to death first."

Amy glanced down at Jim. He looked peaceful. It was something. At least he hadn't suffered. "If Julia can breathe smoke, so can I. Don't worry, Randy. I'll be fine. Help the fat kid and the man. But whatever you do, don't interfere."

Randy let her go. He must have been positive it was Julia who had the upper hand with Frank. Amy wasn't surprised. The only thing that surprised her was that Frank was still alive.

The rear of the store was an inferno. Geysers of dark smoke poured forth on waves of rupturing glass. It was difficult to imagine how either Julia or Frank could still be conscious unless they had brought oxygen tanks to the shootout.

Amy had an answer a moment later. She was only a foot or two into the dense cloud of smoke, when she noticed a sliding wooden door on the right side of the wall. Moving it back an inch, she peeked inside.

"Hello," Julia said matter-of-factly.

The door opened into the office, a space closer to the size of a box than a room. Julia stood in the center of it, with Frank pushed up against the side wall. The finger Julia held to the trigger of the pistol jammed under Frank's jaw was slippery with her sweat. Julia gazed at Amy with calm green eyes, so calm they looked utterly mad.

"Can I come in?" Amy asked.

"No," Julia said.

"Why not?" Frank said. Julia scowled at him, but Frank didn't care. Amy slipped the door open wider and squeezed inside, closing the door quickly at her back, but not quick enough to prevent a barrel of smoke from entering. They were all coughing, and soon they were all going to be frying. The wall Julia had Frank shoved up against was cindering around the edges.

"What are you doing?" Amy asked. "Jim's dead."

"I know he's dead," Julia said flatly, hardly looking at her. Julia had her eyes fixed on Frank's face, which was hardly in picture-perfect shape. Assuming Frank still had a head on his shoulders in the morning, it was going to hurt. He looked as if he had used his face for a battering ram. Amy tried not to look at the meaty pulp that was his right shoulder. Julia had beaten him up pretty good, yet she had taken almost as bad as she had given. Her red hair was streaked with blood, the area around her nose and mouth was turning purple, and part of her ear was blown away.

"You can't kill him," Amy said.

"Sure I can," Julia said.

"You don't know who he is."

"Sure I do."

Amy started to reach for the gun. "Julia."

"Stop," Julia said, and the word came out so cold it froze Amy's hand in midair. Julia tilted her head to the side, apparently listening to the progress of the fire through the store. "You don't have to watch this, Amy."

"I'm not leaving," Amy said. "You're not killing him."

Julia turned toward her and chuckled without mirth. "What about Scott? What about Jim?"

"I didn't kill Jim," Frank interrupted.

Julia slapped him in the face with her free hand. "Shut up!"

"Stop that!" Amy shouted.

"Why?" Julia asked. "He's murdered everyone we love."

"I didn't kill Jim," Frank said again.

Amy was confused. He sounded like he was telling the truth. "Who did?" she asked.

"The store manager accidentally shot Jim," Julia said coolly, barely restraining herself, obviously wanting to slap Frank again and again. "But it was this bastard here that made it all possible."

Amy thought she understood why Julia hadn't killed Frank yet. She was drawing it out, torturing him.

"Do you know who this guy is?" Amy asked.

"Frank," Julia said.

"His full name is Frank Truckwater," Amy said. "He used to go out with a girl named Kary Florence."

"How did you know that?" Frank asked, a vicious twist distorting his already messed-up face. Amy saw she had Julia's attention.

"Who is that?" Julia asked.

"Kary was the girl your mother took care of just before she died," Amy said. "Frank was driving the motorcycle she was on. There was an accident. Kary hurt her head real bad."

"It wasn't my fault," Frank said quickly.

Julia nodded tightly. "My mother talked about it."

"What she didn't talk about was who Kary was," Amy said. "She was your half-sister, Julia."

"Goddamn," Frank whispered, staring at Julia's eyes. He was a believer already. He was the easy one.

"I don't have a half-sister," Julia snapped angrily.

"I talked to your dad," Amy began.

"I don't have a dad!" Julia interrupted. "Why are you here? Get out of here. I have to finish this alone. I won't listen to your lies."

"I'm not lying!" Amy shouted back. "I'm your best friend, in case you forgot that. This jerk here was your sister's best friend. He was drunk. He crashed his—"

"I wasn't drunk!" Frank swore bitterly.

"You were, too, drunk," Amy snapped back at him. "I read the medical record from when you were admitted to the hospital after the accident. The alcohol level in your blood was twice what it takes to be drunk."

"That's a lie!" Frank said.

"You were stoned then and you're stoned now," Amy said, pulling from her back pocket the glass tube she had found in his garage. "What is this?"

"I know what it is," Julia said, swiping the tube from her hand. "He uses it to smoke his ice. So what? So he was stoned?"

"Listen to me, Julia," Amy said. "There's more. Kary was admitted along with Frank. I read her medical report, too. That's how I got her dad's address. I went there. I talked to her dad. He has your eyes, Julia. You have his eyes. Frank can tell you I'm telling the truth. You have the same eyes Kary did!"

Julia was breathing hard. It was a pity she had only smoke to inhale. She pressed her pistol deeper into Frank's throat. "Do I have her eyes?" she asked.

"Pull your goddamn trigger," he said savagely.

"Do I have her eyes?" Julia demanded, close to drilling him.

"I wasn't drunk!" he yelled back. "I only had a few beers. I got run off the road."

"Who ran you off the road?" Julia asked.

"I don't know! Somebody!" He threw his hands in the air, not minding that he shook Julia's trigger finger in the process. "Yeah, you have her eyes. Are you satisfied? Now would you just kill me so I don't have to keep looking at you!"

His remarks threw Julia for a loop. The flames that fueled her anger faltered. Amy could understand why. Now Julia *knew* she'd had a halfsister. She drew her gun back and calmed down somewhat.

"Why did you curse my mother?" Julia asked.

Frank looked suddenly weary. "She said she would heal Kary."

"My mother would never have said such a thing," Julia said.

"Then your dad said it," Frank snapped. "He told me there was hope. Kary woke up for a few minutes. He went to your mother. He talked to her."

"What did they talk about?" Julia asked.

"They didn't tell me," Frank said. "All I know is that when Mr. Florence came back, he acted like Kary was going to live. He was sure of it, even when the doctors still said she was going to die." Frank glared at

170

Julia again. "Kary was awake before your mother got ahold of her."

Julia moved back a step. Again, her expression changed completely. It was as if an unsolvable riddle had at last been explained. A light dawned on her face, yet it cast a shadow. There was no joy for her in the comprehension. "My mother tried to heal my sister," she whispered.

"Well, she did a great job," Frank said bitterly, spitting on the floor. "Kary had a sheet over her face the next time I saw her."

Julia nodded faintly, a faraway look in her eyes. "I was there. I saw her. I saw my sister."

"Julia," Amy said.

Julia turned to Amy. Pain had replaced Julia's madness. Amy continued to marvel at the transformation. And it was Frank's comments that were bringing it about. Yet Amy did not understand what Julia meant when she said she *saw* her sister.

Did Julia see her in a vision?

Did Julia have visions?

"How is Scott?" Julia asked.

Amy shook her head. "He's dying."

"How long does he have?" Julia asked.

"No one knows," Amy said. "Hours. It could be minutes."

"Kary couldn't have had long either," Julia muttered, frowning, confused. "My mother must have helped Kary before she woke up."

"No," Frank said.

"Yes," Julia insisted. "You don't know. She must have tried twice. That's why our dad was sure she was helping her. He must have seen results."

Our dad.

"Your mother was a witch," Frank muttered.

Julia didn't like the comment, but she didn't start screaming at Frank or strike him again, as Amy had expected. But Julia spoke firmly to Frank. "My mother was a great woman. She gave her life to save your girlfriend. What more could she give?" Julia turned to Amy. "Didn't the doctors say that if Scott woke up he'd stand a chance?"

Amy hesitated before answering. She sensed a danger in the question, although she couldn't pinpoint what it was. "Yes," she said.

"That's good, then," Julia answered softly, thoughtfully. She glanced at the gun in her hand. A look of revulsion crossed her features. When she spoke next, it was as if she were addressing herself. "This is not why I'm here, is it?"

"No," Amy said.

Julia glanced up. "But Frank's hurt us all."

"He's been hurt," Amy said. "And he did love your sister."

Julia turned to Frank. "Did you love her?"

Frank was about to snap at her again. Then he stopped. "Yeah, I guess I did," he said reluctantly.

"Did people really run you off the road?" Julia asked.

Frank's lip quivered. "Yeah."

"Tell me," Julia insisted, but it was in a gentle voice. Frank lowered his head.

"I was drunk," he mumbled. "I hit a tree."

"Was anyone else around?" Julia asked.

Frank looked up. "I hit the tree. Kary hit the tree. There was just us and the stupid tree."

Julia nodded, appreciating the truth. "It's hard to say some things."

"It's hard to shoot some people," Frank said, and he was being serious. "Kary couldn't have shot anybody."

Julia smiled faintly. "What was she like?"

"Full of life." Frank nodded to himself.

"Maybe someday we'll talk about her," Julia said, appearing to come to a decision. She stuffed the drug tube in her back pocket and handed the gun to Amy. "Cover him. Don't take your eye off him. Any sudden moves, shoot him. He's still dangerous. The police will probably be here soon." Julia turned to leave.

"Where are you going?" Amy asked. She pointed the gun at Frank.

"To do what I'm here for," Julia said.

"Wait! What is that?"

Julia slid the door open. The smoke that poured in was as hot as a dragon's breath. "Goodbye, Amy."

"Wait. Please? I have to tell you about your father."

Julia paused and glanced over her shoulder. "There's no time."

"He said for you to come to see him. He wants to see you."

Julia nodded. Even the smoke couldn't hide how the sorrow in her face deepened at the mention of her father. "There's no time," she repeated quietly.

Then Julia was gone. Amy couldn't go after her and cover Frank at the same time. Amy motioned Frank into the hallway, and he obeyed without protest. The fight seemed to have gone out of him after he admitted he was to blame for Kary's death. But the heated smoke quickly rose about them, and she might have lost Frank in the thick of it and allowed him to bolt, if Randy hadn't been waiting near the cash register with his shotgun ready. He pointed it at Frank's head, blocking off any possibility of escape.

"Is this the guy?" Randy asked.

"Yeah, watch him," Amy said, scanning the store and the parking lot outside. There was no sign of Julia. "Where'd she go?"

"I don't know," Randy said, rubbing Frank's nose with the tip of the shotgun, much to Frank's displeasure. "But she was in one hell of a hurry, I can tell you that."

"You might want to keep Julia away from him."

"Why?"

"You get nothing for free in this world. Did you know that, Amy?"

What Mr. Florence had been trying to tell her hit Amy like a punch in the gut. He thought Mother Florence had died as a result of trying to heal Kary! It was so obvious! How could she have been so dense not to see that their gift of healing exacted a heavy price? The truth had been staring her in the face from the beginning. When Julia first touched Scott after he had been shot, she said she would die if she touched him again.

Amy coughed. The pain in her eyes and her chest was quickly becoming unbearable. "We have to go after her," she gasped.

"Can't I work this dude over first?" Randy asked, poking the shotgun barrel—none too gently—into Frank's guts. The smoke didn't seem to be bothering either of them as much as it did her. She was confused until she remembered that Randy smoked cigarettes and Frank smoked crystals.

174

"No," Amy said. "We have to go after Julia. She's going to the hospital." Amy staggered around the counter, worried about Jim's body. The smoke was making her dizzy. She wondered if it had alcohol in it, if she was getting intoxicated along with lung cancer. She stuck out a hand on the counter to steady herself. The flames had reached the end of the hallway and had begun to lick the back wall of the store.

"We'll catch up with her," Randy said, still playing his annoying games with Frank.

Amy caught sight of Jim. If they didn't move him soon, there'd be nothing left to bury. There was also the unconscious fat kid, she reminded herself, the one with the minced beef for a knee. The fire was coming for him next. The bottles of booze on the shelves close to the hallway were feeling the heat of the flames. Their labels were peeling away and turning into black ash. The liquids inside sizzled.

I won't let the fire get you, Jim. I won't do that to your parents.

But did she have a choice? Jim and Scott were already lost. If she spent her time in mourning, she could lose Julia as well.

She's going to try to wake Scott up.

"No," Amy said. "We have to go after her now. Now, Randy!"

Randy looked over. "We can't leave this jerk."

"Then we'll take him with us."

"What about Jim? And the kid and owner here?"

Amy had no good answer. Growing frantic, she rounded the counter and reached down to pull on Jim's feet. But a frightening coughing spasm grabbed hold of her then, and she just about spit out pieces of her lungs. Amy staggered back from Jim, feeling weak.

She needed help, she realized. She needed fresh air. "Randy," she moaned.

Just then about a hundred people showed up. No, it wasn't really a hundred, she thought, but it was a lot. They all came at once, like in the space of thirty seconds. First there was Lieutenant Crawley and two of his men. They burst through the front door with their guns drawn, like tough cops in TV shows. They even talked tough.

"Drop it or die!" Lieutenant Crawley shouted at Randy.

"I play on the football team!" Randy shouted back. But he dropped the shotgun and put up his hands. Frank raised his arms as well, although somewhat lackadaisically. He appeared to have been waiting for the cops to show, and now that they were there, he was bored. He no longer looked threatening—the evil, murdering thief. Now he just looked small and useless.

Before Amy could properly respond, Julia's aunt and a couple of the women in black also came through the front door. It was quite a scene—smoke and flames poured from the back as a group of hags faced off against three modern lawmen in blue. Crawley looked at the women as if he was seeing things.

"What are you doing here?" he asked.

"Where's Julia Florence?" the aunt demanded, ignoring him.

"I have no idea," Crawley said. "Who the hell are you?"

"I'm her aunt," the woman said. She caught the lieutenant's eye. "Where is she?"

Crawley stared at her a second, then shook his head. "I don't know. I don't know nothing."

The aunt looked over at Amy. Even though the mass of smoke, Amy could see the violet in her eyes, and feel the strength in their depths. The aunt's question felt to Amy as if it had been psychically drilled into her mind.

Where is my niece? Tell me now or I'll cut out your tongue!

But all the aunt said out loud was, "Do you know where Julia is?"

"No," Amy said, stumbling against the counter, trying to resist the mental pull of the woman. "Leave her alone. Leave me alone."

"Where is she?" the aunt insisted. "She's not here."

"I don't know," Amy said, shaking her head, trying not to look at the woman.

The aunt watched her like a hawk. Then she slowly nodded, apparently having gotten what she wanted. "It's true, Amy," she said in an odd tone Amy didn't understand. "We both know." The aunt turned and snapped at the two who followed her, "Come on."

Amy tried to go after them. But Lieutenant Crawley stopped her. "Hold on a second, young lady," he said.

Another coughing fit struck Amy. This forced her to double up. "I have to get outside," she gasped. "So does Randy. We're both innocent."

Crawley thought for a moment. Then he took pity on her. "Don't go far," he said. Then he called to his men, gesturing to Randy and Frank. "Get cuffs on those two. Take them outside and read them their rights."

Amy managed to straighten herself, although she was unable to properly catch her breath. She nodded behind the counter. "My boyfriend's body is on the floor there," she whispered. "Take care of it. Please?"

Crawley nodded. He patted her on the back. "Get outside, girl. Get some fresh air. Adams, I changed my mind. Let the jock go. He plays for Indian Pole's football team. He's harmless."

"Thanks a lot," Randy said, insulted. One of the officers unlocked the cuffs he had just snapped on Randy's wrists. Randy helped Amy to the door. Breathing was an ordeal for her. Even the fresh air outside hurt to inhale. She hung onto Randy and directed him around the side of the liquor store.

Her car was gone.

"Julia must have taken it," Randy said.

Amy shook her head. "No," she mumbled, although she knew it was true.

"Well, it's not here," Randy replied, glancing about the parking lot. "At least I don't see it."

"We have to stop her. She'll die."

"Julia? Nah. She's made of steel. Nothing can kill her."

"She's going to kill herself." Amy had to lean against the wall. She saw that the aunt's car was already gone. "We need a car, Randy."

"The only car here is that cop car. I don't think they'd appreciate us taking it."

"Are they all still inside?" Amy asked.

"Yeah."

"Look and see if they left the keys in the ignition."

"Are you serious?"

Amy spat out a mouthful of ash mixed with saliva. "Do I look serious?"

Randy nodded. "I'll have a look."

Amy tried to draw herself erect once more, but she ended up slumping to the ground. Her head rolled back on her shoulders, and she could see the stars in the sky overhead. Glimpsed through the fiery orange glow, they made her feel as if she were back in a primeval world, beside an erupting volcano. She would have liked to go back in time, she thought, even a single day. She missed Jim already.

Don't think about him. Think about him later. Julia is all that matters now.

Amy realized that, no matter how much she loved Scott, she was unwilling to risk Julia to save him. The way things were going, she knew she would just lose them both.

Randy was back in a moment. "The keys are in the ignition, Amy."

She stuck out her arm. "Good. Help me up and put me behind the steering wheel."

"We'll go to jail if we steal this thing."

"They'll have to catch us first."

Shaking his head, Randy knelt down and picked her up. He carried her to the cop car, which was parked close to the road. "I'll drive," he said.

"No."

"You're in no condition to hit the road," he said firmly.

Not only were the keys still in the ignition of the cop car, the engine was running. When Randy opened the passenger side, Amy slid down and collapsed in the front seat. Randy jumped behind the steering wheel and eagerly rubbed his hands together.

"I've always wanted to drive one of these babies," he confessed.

Randy floored the accelerator, and they left two trails of rubber behind.

The hospital was approximately twenty-five miles from the liquor store, but the road was narrow and windy. Randy almost sent them into the trees half a dozen times. Amy rolled down the window and drank deeply of the fresh, cold night air. It was not long before her coughing began to subside and her head cleared.

Rounding a turn, Amy noticed a station wagon up ahead. "Is that who I think it is in front of us?" she asked.

Randy nodded. "It's those ugly women. What do you want to do?"

Amy glanced in the backseat, hoping to see an extra police uniform. There was only a blue cap and a billy club.

"Put on the siren," she said.

Randy loved the idea. "I've been wanting to do it, but I thought you'd yell at me." He flipped a switch beside the CB. The red light on the roof flickered against the trees that lined the road, and the siren blared into the night. "Somebody in town must have had points that fit that wagon," Randy muttered.

Amy watched as the old women put on their brakes. "Are you game to stop them again?" she asked.

"Sure."

"It'll mean being left behind."

Randy immediately grasped what she had in mind. He wasn't as stupid as he pretended. "Do I get to play cop?" he asked.

"Exactly." Amy reached in the back for the cap and billy club. She also found a pair of sunglasses and a powerful flashlight in the glove compartment. The car up ahead pulled to the side of the road and stopped. "Here, put on this stuff. The sunglasses, too. You'll probably only be able to stop them for a few seconds.

But if you keep the flashlight in their eyes—like real cops do—you might be able to extend the time."

Randy shook his head and reached for the shotgun racked between the seats. "I'm going to stop them for a lot longer than a few seconds."

"You can't shoot them," Amy said, aghast.

Randy began to slow. "I can shoot their tires if they don't do what I say."

"That's pretty dramatic."

Randy shrugged. "If it's to help Julia, what the hell." He put on the cap and the glasses. The aunt's car was only a hundred yards up ahead. He slowed to a crawl. "I can hardly see with these damn things on."

"They look good on you," Amy said, scooting down in the seat so the women wouldn't see her before she had a chance to drive away. Randy glanced over at her.

"I'm sorry about Jim," he said. "I shouldn't have said the things I did. He was a hell of a football player."

"Thanks."

"Are you going to be all right without me?"

"I'll be fine." Amy reached over and squeezed his hand. "You've been great, Randy. I really mean it."

Randy sighed. "If only we'd got there a few minutes earlier."

Amy remembered how she had tried to warn Jim on the phone to stay away from Julia.

She was worried about you, not Scott. It was you she stopped from going in the gas station.

"Maybe it was meant to be," she said sadly.

Randy parked a few seconds later. He trained the cop car's side light on the old women and stuffed the billy club in his belt. He pumped the police shotgun as he opened the door. "Don't drive off until you hear me talking to them," he said.

"I won't," she said, ready to slide over into the driver's seat. Randy had left the engine running. "Don't look too closely in the aunt's eyes."

"Tell me about it," Randy said. "Goodbye, babe."

"Good luck," she whispered.

Randy got out and strode toward the old women. Amy immediately slid over, keeping her head low, but not so low that she couldn't peek over the steering wheel. The way Randy swaggered up to the window brought a smile to her face. He walked just like a cop. He shone the flashlight directly in the driver's eyes, whom Amy assumed was the aunt. Even if the old woman was a master hypnotist, Amy doubted she could see a thing. Randy held his shotgun in the other hand and put on a redneck southern accent.

"In a hurry tonight, are we, ladies?" he said. "Let me see your license and registration."

The women seemed to fall for the disguise, at least for the moment. Amy saw one of them, lit up in Randy's beam, search the glove compartment for the papers. There was no point in staying any longer, she thought. She sat up and quickly shifted into drive, flooring the accelerator. She tore around Randy and the women, sending up a cloud of dust. The aunt must have understood in a second what was going on. In the rearview mirror, Amy saw the woman behind the wheel restart the car and floor her own gas pedal. Randy was forced to jump back, but he hadn't been caught off guard. Before they could get thirty feet, he put a couple of shots in their rear tires. The car skidded off the road, back onto the gravel shoulder.

The last thing Amy saw, before she went around a bend and lost sight of them, was three old women jumping out of the car and running toward Randy.

I hope the aunt doesn't change him into a toad.

Then again, Julia could probably kiss him and change him back.

Chapter Fifteen

IT was past midnight when Julia arrived at the hospital. The hallways were all but deserted. She was glad for that. Taking a quick stop in the restroom, what she saw in the mirror led her to believe that the first doctor she passed in the corridor would want to treat her. Frank had definitely done a number on her right ear. Half the lower lobe was missing, and what was left looked none too pretty. Both her eyes were purple. A bruise the size of a baseball was poking out from the center of her forehead, and her hair looked as if it had been dipped in a can of red paint.

When I walk into intensive care, I'll tell them I belong there. That I just got up to go to the bathroom and got lost for a couple of days.

Julia wished she could at least find a bandage for her ear. She could hide the mess beneath her hair, but the strands kept brushing against the torn tissue, making her feel nauseated. In fact, before Julia left the restroom, she vomited. There was too much ugliness in her head. The kid's knee exploding. Jim's white jacket turning to red. Frank's bitter sneer. Yet those things weren't the only source of her nausea. Bent over the toilet bowl, the contents of her stomach already gone, Julia realized that she was no better than Frank, that she was worse in a way. She had wonderful gifts and all she had managed to use them for was to bring other people pain.

"What would your mother say?"

Her mother wouldn't have said anything. She wouldn't have complained. She would just have done what she thought was right, and let God worry about the consequences.

"People are responsible for their actions, but not the fruits of their actions. Always do what you think is right, but don't worry if good does not always come from what you do."

Kneeling on the floor beside the toilet, Julia lowered her head and prayed. She prayed for the courage to do what she knew she should have done from the beginning, since the first shot had been fired, but she didn't have her mother's courage. She also prayed that she wouldn't die doing this thing.

Finally Julia stood and left the cubicle. She washed her face in the sink. She needed a plan. She couldn't just waltz into intensive care, no matter how beat up she looked. It was late, but there would still be at least one nurse on duty, and she needed to be alone with Scott.

Julia had only stepped out of the bathroom when she spotted Sally Hanlon. She recognized the waitress, of course, from the football game, when the woman had slugged Scott with her bag. Scott had told her a bit about Sally. But the woman didn't recognize Julia. Sally had a cake box in hand, and she didn't even pause as she passed Julia in the hall. Julia suspected Sally was there to visit Scott, the late hour notwithstanding. Sally was heading in the direction of intensive care.

"Hi," Julia said.

Sally stopped. "What happened to you, dearie?"

"I got mugged."

"Oh, you poor thing! Have you seen a doctor yet?"

"No. I'll see one soon. You're here to see Scott, aren't you?"

"Yeah, I am," Sally said. "Are you a friend of Scott's?"

"Yes. I saw you at the game with him."

"Really?" Sally paused. "How old are you?"

"Seventeen."

Sally sighed. "You're the youngest one yet. Do you know Randy Classick?"

"Yes."

"Well, that jerk was supposed to be at my house hours ago, but he never showed. Do you know where he is?"

"The last time I saw him, he was at the liquor store on Barnes, by the lake."

Sally was disgusted. "Getting himself something to get drunk on, I bet."

"No. He was trying to put out a fire."

"Come again, honey?"

"Never mind." Julia glanced at Sally's cake box. "Did Randy tell you that Scott was in the hospital?"

"Yeah. When Randy didn't come over, I thought I'd mosey on down and visit with Scott. I brought him a chocolate cake from the diner." Sally glanced at her watch. "But I suppose it might be kind of late for socializing."

186

"Did Randy tell you what's wrong with Scott?"

Sally wasn't as dull as she appeared. She looked up sharply, concern in her heavily painted eyes. "No. He just said Scott was sick. What's wrong with him?"

"He's been shot in the head. He's in a coma right now. The doctors say he's going to die."

Sally paled and put her hand to her mouth. "Oh Lord, the poor child! Randy didn't tell me none of this. Can't we do something for him?"

Julia took a step closer to the woman. She spoke seriously. "I can. But I have to be alone with him. I need your help."

Sally was confused. "What are you going to do?"

For a moment, Julia wished she had her aunt's power to influence people by the power of her eyes and voice alone. It sure would have come in handy right then. On the other hand, her own cleverness and Sally's good nature might serve just as well. Along with a good dose of the truth.

"Do you believe that there's healing power in love?" Julia asked sincerely.

Sally nodded. "I know that when I have a man in my life who loves me, I never catch a cold or the flu. Is that what you mean, child?"

"Yes. Scott's one of my oldest friends. We've known each other since we were kids. But there are things I've never told him—personal things. I want to tell him those things now. I believe that, even though he's in a coma, he'll be able to hear me, and that these things will help him. Does that make sense?"

Sally looked her over slowly. "You love him a lot, don't ya?"

"I sure do."

Sally nodded. "Scott's a good kid. I could see that

from the start, even if he lied to me about his age. How can I help you?"

Julia had driven Amy's car to the hospital. She hadn't had time to go for Scott's when she dashed from the liquor store. But it was Amy's car that had Scott's camcorder in it. While Scott had been on the operating table, Amy had removed it from Scott's car because she was afraid Scott's parents would see his cheerleader tape. Scott's mother was very conservative. Julia had noticed the camcorder on the floor of the front seat only a few minutes earlier.

"Could you come to the parking lot with me for a minute?" Julia asked. "I want to show you something."

"Sure," Sally said.

The moon was straight overhead now, dyeing the surrounding woods a soft lustrous silver. Julia led Sally to Amy's car. Julia suspected Amy knew what she was up to and that she was not far behind. Time was of the essence. Julia took out the camcorder and handed it to Sally.

"Do you know how to work one of these?" Julia asked.

Sally studied the instrument. "Don't you just push this little button here?"

"Yeah, that's good enough. The red light will come on. You don't need to worry about focusing. It does it automatically."

Sally was confused again. "Are we going to be making a movie?"

"Sort of. I told you that I need to be alone with Scott, but there'll be a nurse on duty. Now, that's my problem. I need you to get her out of the way. I want you to pretend you're from a local news station and that you're doing a special on how hard the county's nurses work. You'll take this camcorder and tell the nurse you want to film her in the corridor, outside intensive care. Tell her she's going to be on TV. Everybody wants to be on TV. She'll be delighted. Do you understand?"

"What's a camcorder?" Sally asked.

"That's what you're holding in your hand."

"Oh."

"You're going to have to act all bubbly, like a TV personality."

"Scott told me the night I met him that he thought I could be on TV," Sally said, getting excited about the scheme.

"You'd be a natural," Julia remarked. Scott always told women he hoped to make nude videos of that they were star material. "Keep her in the hallway as long as you can."

"Gotcha."

"I really appreciate you doing all this for me, Sally."

"It's my pleasure. Who mugged you?"

"The person who shot Scott."

"Really?" Sally's face darkened. "You should go to the police."

"The police already have the guy in custody. Look, I was serious about needing as much time as you can get me."

Sally looked up at the moon. "I believe a person should be able to say goodbye to someone the way they want. I'll take that nurse for coffee if I have to. And who knows, child—maybe your love will bring Scott back to life."

"Maybe it will," Julia said.

They went back inside. Julia waited down the hall, while Sally entered the intensive-care ward. Perhaps Sally was ready for prime time after all. Julia could have sworn the woman was in there less than a minute when she emerged with not one but two nurses. Sally quickly diverted them away from the entrance door, chatting all the time about the great work the nurses of Idaho were doing compared to the rest of the country and the high ratings the *network* expected to get on the program. Julia didn't mind that Sally had changed her persona from a local to a national reporter. Moving swiftly but silently, Julia slipped into intensive care and made her way to Scott's cubicle, relieved to find no other personnel on duty.

To the average observer, Scott would have appeared little different from the previous night. His head bandages had been changed and were no longer stained with blood, but otherwise he looked the same—shockingly pale, perfectly motionless, and with enough tubes and wires to qualify him as terminal. Yet to Julia, there was one significant change.

The previous night, when Amy had questioned her about Scott's condition, Julia had told Amy that his light was weak. She had spoken from direct perception. Julia did not see auras in the sense some of her mother's relatives did. She did not see elaborate patterns of colors around people from which emotions and secret desires could be divined. But she could see, on occasion, the energy field that surrounded all living things, particularly when she was viewing them in her pond. She had needed no pond last night, however, to see that Scott's aura had shrunk to a faint blur that didn't even encompass his head. And now that feeble glow was all but gone. Julia glanced at the EEG screen above his bed. His brain-wave activity, depicted by a series of four lines of green light, was practically flat.

"Oh, Scott," Julia said, wiping away a tear. "You're never going to get to Tahiti in this condition."

There were three chairs in the corner of the cubicle, and Julia pulled one close to the bed, near Scott's head, and sat down. She reminded herself that Sally couldn't keep the nurses long, but still she hesitated before touching him. She was afraid. The black tidal wave of her earlier attempt to heal him appeared before her inner eye, and with it came the poisonous vapors. Intent upon killing Frank, the smoke inside the burning liquor store had hardly troubled her, but the mere thought of these etheric fumes made her choke. They were connected with death, she knew, in all forms. It was no coincidence that her first vision of the future in the moonlight had also been thick with smoke.

But now, with her resolution to heal Scott, she had to ask herself if she wasn't once again moving against the currents of *what was meant to be*. Perhaps she was only compounding her earlier sin—she didn't know. Yet her mother's words came back to reassure her. She could only try to do what she felt was right. If God didn't like it, then at least he would understand. Julia bowed her head and prayed the simplest of all prayers.

Be with me, God. Stay with me.

Then Julia sat up and put her left hand on Scott's left hand and her right hand on the top of his head. She concentrated on nothing in particular. She was sitting beside her friend, and he was hurt. All she wanted was for him to be well again.

Julia closed her eyes and took a deep breath.

As she exhaled, the breath went out of her body. Julia slumped forward across Scott's chest.

Julia was walking in the woods with her mother. The day was bright and warm, and they were looking for herbs. A soft breeze rustled the leaves and played with Julia's long hair. The birds in the nearby branches were full of song, and her mother sang with them. Julia was happy, yet she knew something about the setting was wrong. She stopped her mother.

"Where are we?" she asked.

Her mother smiled. "Home."

Julia frowned and surveyed her surroundings. "I don't recognize any of these trees. Why is that?"

"Because you've never come this deep into the woods before. Don't you remember the way we came?" Her mother indicated a path behind them.

Julia shook her head. "I don't remember."

"Tell me what you do remember," her mother said gently.

Julia rubbed her head. "My head feels funny."

"Why does it feel funny?"

"I don't know, Mom."

"What is the last thing you remember?" her mother repeated.

Julia thought for a moment. "I was at school. The principal came and called me into his office. Amy came with me. He told me something—I can't remember what it was. But I got worried about you. I got in my car and drove home as fast as I could. I ran into the woods, looking for you." Julia wrinkled her forehead. "Are you all right?"

"I'm fine."

Julia smiled, although she was still confused. "That's good."

Her mother indicated the path behind them once more. "Don't you want to see the way you came?"

Julia eyed the path uneasily. It led into a thickly shadowed part of the woods. It was much brighter where they were standing, and Julia saw no reason to move. The sunlight on her bare arms felt wonderfully reassuring.

"Not really," she told her mother.

"What if I came with you?"

"Why do I have to go back when I just got here?"

"Because you left school a few minutes too early."

"OK," Julia said, even though she was not sure what her mother meant. Her mother offered her hand, and Julia took it. They started back along the path. Soon they had moved into the thick shade, and the sun vanished. Yet Julia felt no fear with her mother beside her.

Until they came to the lake.

"Do you know where we are now?" her mother asked as they stopped near the water. The sun was in the sky once more, shining down on both of them, yet Julia had the distinct impression that now it was only shining on her mother. It was as if the sky had drawn a curtain over Julia's head.

Julia shivered. The air was cold, and she knew the lake would be even colder. She had no desire to stand beside it. She remembered that Scott had almost drowned in it. She mentioned the incident to her mother, and although she knew she had never told her mother about it before, her mother nodded as if she knew all about the time Scott had cramped.

"You almost died when you tried to rescue him," her mother said. She held up her fingers, a fraction of an inch apart. "You came that close."

"Were you there?"

Her mother took a seat on the shore. "I don't know. I guess not."

"Then how did you know?"

Her mother picked up a stick and began to draw on the white sand that led to the water. "I know you, Julia. You're my daughter. You would do anything for anybody. You let Scott have the rope first, even when you felt your own muscles begin to fail."

"Scott must have told you. Or Amy told you. Is that it?"

Her mother continued to draw with her stick. "I told Amy about you. About your gifts."

"Why? You said we had to keep them secret."

"I knew one day you'd need her help."

"Amy's? When?"

"Today."

"What is today?" Julia began to ask, when she noticed that her mother was not drawing in the sand but writing. It was a word, one word. *Hospital.* "Hospital," Julia whispered, and suddenly she remembered *everything.* The liquor store. The gas station. Her half-sister. The motorcycle accident and the cerebral hemorrhage. Julia felt weak. "You're dead, Mom," she said.

Her mother nodded, gazing over the serene lake. "In a way, I suppose. But everybody's day eventually comes, and life still goes on. The flower bud dies, but the rose blooms. It's a mystery." She smiled and shook her head. "It's pretty here. I don't feel dead."

Julia knelt by her side. "Where are we? Am I dead, too?"

Her mother took her hand and looked directly in her eyes. Her mother did not have the power of her aunt to force people to do things against their will. But she had an inner strength that flowed out through her eyes. It gave people the will to accomplish what *they* wanted to do.

"No, Julia," she said. "You're still alive. But you've taken a step out of life, and I've taken a step toward it, to meet you here. You're trying to do something beyond your power. You can't heal Scott, not by yourself."

Julia glanced toward the flat surface of the lake. There were no ripples, yet there was no reflection from the neighboring trees. The lake existed in the woods, but it was not a part of the woods. The surface shone like a mirror placed in an empty sky. The lake held a special fear for her—because once she almost drowned there. That was why her mother had led her there.

"I need your help," Julia said.

"You need God's help."

Julia turned back to her mom. "But I've already asked for it."

"That's true. But you asked without knowing what you were asking. No one can bring back the dead, Julia. Only God can do that."

"But Scott isn't dead."

"I'm not talking about Scott."

Julia froze, then nodded slowly. "I will die if I try to help him."

"Yes. You had your suspicions. They are true." Her mother let go of her stick, and it fell to the ground beside the word she had carved out. "It's a hard decision to make."

Julia felt as if the sun had vanished from the sky. Yet when she looked up, it was still there, even though it felt as if the last ray of warmth was drained from it. She began to tremble as she had when Amy finally pulled her to shore, half-drowned, half-frozen.

"I thought I already made my decision," Julia said.

"You did."

"Then why am I here? Why are you asking me to make it again?"

Her mother looked away. "It's so wonderful to have you beside me again. You know that?"

"I've missed you terribly," Julia said.

Her mother nodded. "But we could be together in another time, one farther off. Do you understand?"

"Yes. You brought me here. You want me to reconsider my decision."

Her mother clasped Julia's hands. "It wasn't your fault Scott was shot. It wasn't your fault you looked into the future. I knew one day you would try it. The moment you did, your powers began to increase—you noticed that. Your aunt may blame you and think you have upset the natural course, but these things happen. You have acted blindly, impulsively, with vengeance blazing in your heart. That was a mistake. When you do something because you're angry, you almost always do the wrong thing. But we learn from our mistakes. We learn when we are acting blindly. But even a blind man pauses when he finally approaches the edge of a lake, Julia. He feels the water; he does not have to see it. He knows when it is too deep to cross."

"I don't understand."

"To heal Scott, not only will you have to give up your life, you will have to drown, as you almost drowned that day. Only that way will you truly understand the consequences of your decision."

Julia was aghast. "But why does it have to be so horrible?"

"Because of another wish you have prayed for."

"What is that?"

"To be with me again," her mother said. "You have a death wish, Julia. When you went after Frank, you didn't care if you died. It is the same with your desire to heal Scott. You would throw your life away on anything."

"That's not true!" Julia cried. "I love Scott. How can you say that, Mom?"

"Because that's the way it is."

"It's not! I came to the hospital to help."

"Who?"

"Scott! Mother, you're twisting how I feel."

Her mother grimaced. She patted Julia's hand again. "I'm sorry I have to say these things. I would just as soon sit here in the sun with you and talk about the flowers we could pick, or the songs we could sing. I know what's in your heart. I've already said you would sacrifice anything to help someone. But sometimes the deepest sacrifices we make are really for ourselves."

"Are you talking about the time you tried to heal Kary?"

Her mother closed her eyes briefly. "Yes. I tried too hard, I think."

"Why did you do it?"

Her mother opened her eyes and looked up at the sun. "I felt I owed your father something. He had given me you, but he never got to see you. Then Kary was lying there on the hospital bed, and he was begging for me to help her. . . ." Her mother shook her head. "I found it impossible to say no."

"Why did he leave us?"

Her mother nodded. "I suppose I felt guilty, too. He left because he had an affair with another woman. She became pregnant with Kary. He didn't love the other woman. He loved me; I know he did. But he couldn't bear my silence on the subject." Her mother shrugged. "I didn't say anything because I didn't know what to say. But just a word from me might have made a difference. I suppose I was mad at him, after all."

"You never got mad."

"People would say the same thing about you, until yesterday. But your anger came from somewhere, Julia, and it was me. I wasn't perfect when I was alive. I'm not perfect now. I can't tell you what to do. A part of me longs for you to stay by my side. The other part can't bear to see the world deprived of your grace."

"But what about Scott?" Julia asked.

Her mother sighed. "I always liked that boy."

"Mom, you didn't just try to heal Kary because you felt guilty. I saw you with her after Frank cursed you. I saw you crying. You thought of her as your own daughter, didn't you?"

Her mother smiled wistfully. "I suppose."

"Well, I feel that way about Scott. He's been chasing me since we were kids, but I've always felt like he was my brother. It's true—I do have a morbid streak in me. I feel like I don't belong in the world. I know it's wrong, but I can't help it. But Scott loves his life. Everything's a joy for him. I think he's the one who will grace people's lives, not me."

Her mother was silent for a long time. Finally she gestured to the lake. "It's cold. It's deep."

"I know." Julia gazed over the flat surface, remembering her nightmare. "Does it have a monster in its depths?"

"You're sure about what you've decided?" her mother asked.

Julia hesitated. "Yes."

Her mother leaned over and hugged her. "Then you will have to see for yourself, my daughter. I can't help you."

Julia understood. She kissed her mother goodbye, stood up, and walked to the end of the shore, where she touched her toe to the still surface. A faint ripple spread out from her foot, yet there remained no reflection to disturb. The water felt like ice, but she took a step forward, feeling the cold sink into her heart. She was not dreaming. She was not outside her body. Life pumped in her veins, in her warm blood, and it screamed for her to stop, with each step that she took. The water reached her waist. It touched her breasts. It climbed to her mouth even, before she started to swim toward the center of the lake.

But she never reached the center. Her muscles began to harden halfway out, to cramp into useless knots, as they had long ago. Her chin slipped beneath the surface, and a mouthful of water got sucked down the wrong tube. She began to cough, to choke, and she fought to stay afloat, even though she had only moments ago chosen to drown. It was impossible not to fight. It was impossible to comprehend the horror that swept over her in that instant. Yet Julia realized something very clearly then, just before she went under.

It was possible to have a death wish and not want to die.

She had leapt after Frank, but if just one of his shots had laid open her guts, she would have sat down and reconsidered. She wanted to reconsider now, to scream for her mother to save her. But a final, frantic glance toward the shore showed her that her mother had disappeared. The water went over Julia's wide-open eyes, the cold biting down on her optic nerves and sending ice daggers into her brain. She sucked in another breath, but this one was pure liquid, worse than the deadliest smoke. She kicked toward the surface with all her strength, but her limbs hardly budged. Sorry, they said, we have turned to stone. We are dead rocks, and we're going to drag you down with us for putting us in this godforsaken lake.

Julia began to sink.

Down she went, deeper and deeper, until the cold sun above the icy surface turned to a dying star shining through a gray atmosphere onto a black world. She could not scream, she could not move. Her diaphragm, which drove her lungs, went into an insane convulsion, with nothing to pump into her insides but water the coldest fish would have refused. Then suddenly it stopped, practically wrenching her in two. Her heart almost stopped then, too. It would have if it weren't for the white light that began to shine beneath her. It was a weird light to have at the bottom of a lake. It was like the quality of light found in an office building or hospital room. She knew God was not waiting for her on the other side of it.

It was fluorescent light.

Julia hit the bottom and rolled over, face down.

Hospital.

The word her mother had written in the sand.

The floor of the lake was made of clear glass. The floor of the lake was also doubling as the new roof of the intensive-care cubicle where Scott and she lay dying. Julia was so amazed that she almost forgot her agony. Sitting off to the side of their two unconscious bodies was a second Scott. He looked as if he were waiting for something to happen, anything. He was dressed exactly as he had been when he entered the gas station.

Julia tried to call to him to get his attention. It was difficult, being underwater. She tried pounding on the glass, which was even more difficult, since she couldn't move. Oh, but there was a part of her body that had a spark of life left in it. Julia flexed her neck back, then snapped it forward. She struck the glass with her head. It was funny—it didn't hurt. She didn't even know if she broke it. But suddenly she was inside, inside looking out.

She was in the hospital but outside her body.

"What are you doing here?" Scott asked.

They were sitting on the two chairs in the corner of the cubicle, looking at their sorry physical selves. Everything seemed to be fairly normal, except each of them had a silver cord trailing off their bodies. The cords were attached at their solar plexuses. Julia's was thick and glowing. Scott's was thin and pale.

"Scott!" Julia cried. "How are you?"

"You should know. You heard what the doctor said."

"You were watching us?" Julia asked, amazed.

He shrugged. "There's nothing else to do right now." He gestured toward his cord. "I think this thing's got to fall off before I can move around."

"No," she said quickly. "If that thing falls off, you're dead."

He didn't appear overly concerned. "I'd say that's a given already, Julia. I watched the operation they performed on me. My brain is scrambled."

"But you can get better. I can help you."

"How?"

She paused. "That's funny: I don't know what I'm supposed to do."

Scott looked vaguely confused. "Hey, what are you doing here, anyway? Why did you pass out when you sat beside me?"

"You saw that, too?"

"Yeah. I thought you came to kiss me goodbye. How come you didn't kiss me goodbye last night? I could have died during the night, you know."

"I was in a hurry."

He was mildly insulted. Everything about him was fairly mild. "But I've known you a long time, Julia. A kiss would have been nice."

"I was anxious to catch the guys who shot you."

"Oh, yeah. How did that go?"

"We caught them. Jim and I did."

"Did you blow them away?"

"I shot the fat kid's knee off. The police probably have the other guy about now."

Scott nodded his approval. "Can't have guys like that running loose. A couple of troublemakers. They wrecked my Friday night, that's for sure."

"Scott? Can I ask you something?"

"Sure."

"How come you don't seem upset about getting shot in the head?"

He had to think for a minute. "I was at first. When I was floating above my body in the gas station, I was freaking out. I never liked the sight of blood—particularly my own. By the way, that was a great move you put on that one guy, dodging his bullet. But then I began to calm down after you touched my head and the angel flew by."

"What angel?" Julia asked.

"I don't know. She didn't tell me her name. She said, Just hang in there, Scotty boy, and don't worry. So that's what I've been doing." He flexed his arm. "You know, this new body here is great. It doesn't get excited about anything. I never even have to go to the bathroom. I just sit here grooving." He paused. "Hey, you didn't answer my question. What are you doing here? How come you're out of your body?"

"I'm here to heal you."

Scott smiled. "Still trying to get my pants off, huh?"

"I never tried to get your pants off."

"Did you get Jim's off?"

She was offended. "What are you talking about?"

Scott continued to smile. "I saw the way you two looked at each other when you met. Do you know what I thought to myself? There goes another one of Amy's boyfriend's down the drain. Poor Amy—she lines them up for herself, and Julia knocks them down. Did Jim try to kiss you later on?"

"No!" She lowered her voice. "Jim's dead. He got killed when we went after the guys who shot you."

"Really?"

She grimaced. "It was horrible."

"I wouldn't worry about it. I'm sure he'll be all right."

"Scott! I told you, he's dead. Jim's dead."

Scott shrugged. "It happens to the best of us. But that's pretty neat—he died trying to get back at them for what they did to me. Jim's a cool guy. If I see him, I've got to thank him."

Julia shook her head. "I don't think you know what the hell's going on here."

Scott wasn't offended. "Am I missing something?"

"Yes! You're about to die."

"I know that. We already talked about that. Is there something else?"

"But you can't die. I don't want you to die."

Scott gestured to his ruined body on the bed. "It doesn't look too good from here. Can't fix a bullet in the head with a bottle of pills. Hey, what do you think of all those tubes they got running into me? You know, they even got one for me to pee in. I saw this real cute nurse changing my bottle. She was blond. I wonder what she thought of my—"

"Scott! Stop! We've got to talk."

"What would you like to talk about?"

"I'm here to heal you. I'm serious. I'm a witch."

He chuckled. "Where's your broom?"

"I don't have one."

"What kind of witch are you?"

"I'm a good witch. That's how I was able to get outside my body right now to talk to you."

Her remark gave him cause to consider. "You're not pulling my leg, are you?"

"No. Do you see any of your other friends sitting here talking to you?"

"You've got a point there." He stared at her still form, and the first trace of anxiety disturbed his features. "Are you all right?"

"Yeah, I'm fine."

He was relieved, slightly. Mild and slight. They could have been talking about bad weather approaching. "Have you always been a witch?" he asked.

"Yes. My mother was also a witch. She could heal people. I can heal people, too, sort of. I can also see things far off when I look in water with the sun shining on it. I even saw the future once. That's how I knew we were going to run into a holdup."

"I remember," he said, showing some excitement. "You didn't want us stopping at any liquor stores. That's neat that you knew what was going to happen. Why didn't you tell us?"

"You wouldn't have believed me."

"I might have. You never know."

"You don't believe me now."

He gave her a sweet look. "Sure I do. I always knew you had magic."

She was touched. "You did?"

"I did. I thought you were an angel, walking around in a body that wouldn't quit."

It was her turn to chuckle. "It's a shame we didn't get to go to Tahiti together. We could have gone swimming naked."

His interest was increasing rapidly. "Would you really have gone skinny-dipping with me?"

"Absolutely."

"That's incredible. You should have told me this before I got shot. I would have been more careful where I stuck my head." He laughed. "Of course, you probably would have ended up saving me from drowning again. I'm so out of shape. I've got to lose weight. I wonder if comas are any good for that. I noticed they've put me on a strict liquid diet."

"Keep me from drowning again."

"Scott!" she exclaimed suddenly.

"Don't shout. This is a hospital."

"I've got it. I know how to heal you. It's the rope. I let you take the rope before. I've got to give you the rope again."

"What are you talking about?"

She pointed to her silver cord. "I've got to give you this."

He didn't think that was a good idea. "It looks better attached to you. Besides, you don't want mine. It looks like its batteries are about to run out."

"That's because you're about to die."

"Are we back on that subject again? I told you I understand that."

"No, you don't understand. You don't have to die."

Scott gazed at her for a moment. His casualness disappeared. "If you give me your cord, Julia, you'll die. I know how it works. The cord connects you to your body. If you don't have it, you don't get to keep your body. I can't let you do that."

"But that's what I'm here for," Julia said. "Look, it's already decided. I've talked to my mother about it and everything. You're going to take my silver cord."

"I don't want it."

"But if you die, you won't get to go to Tahiti."

"I don't want to go if I can't go with you," Scott said.

"Goddamnit, listen to me!"

"Don't swear. They might not let us into heaven."

"You used to swear all the time!" she swore at him.

Scott lowered his head. "Why should I get to stay and you have to go? I don't think it's fair."

She softened her tone. "It's not what's fair that matters, Scott. It's what was meant to be. I see that now. When I saw the future, the holdup, I was outside my body. I think that's because I was seeing my own death. I'm supposed to be here, on this side of the mirror. It's where I feel most at home. You're supposed to be in your body. You have screenplays to write and movies to film. You have girls to love. You have all these things to look forward to."

"What about you?"

Julia looked upward. There was no glass ceiling, no icy lake floor above them. Suddenly she felt certain that if she took one final step, she would never have to sink into such cold depths ever again. She would fly upward, higher than the greatest bird, beyond the sky, where the sun never set, and where it was always warm.

But only if I take the step in love. Mom told me I can't just want to escape.

"I've had a happy life," she said. "I've walked in the woods in the morning. I've had friends. I've been in love."

"With who?" Scott asked.

"With you. I love you, Scott. You know that."

"How come you never wanted to have sex with me?"

She smiled. "Because I was afraid I would get pregnant, and then there would be two of you. And there can only be one Scott. There *has* to be one Scott. The world needs you." She took his hand, and placed it on her forehead. "Take the rope, Scott. I gave it to you before and you took it. Take it now, and breathe, and live, and write a story about me. Take it because you deserve it, because I'm not going to leave until you do. I'll stay here until we both die."

He was watching her closely. "You're serious?"

"Yes."

"I still don't think it's fair."

"No. But it's right. That's what matters."

"It will break Amy's heart if you die."

"She'll understand." Julia reached over and hugged him. "Tell her goodbye for me."

Scott hugged her in return. "Will I remember any of this?"

Julia sat back and focused on his eyes. She prayed to God to be able to do this one last thing, to have a portion of her aunt's magic. She reached out with her heart to put the thought deep in Scott's mind, while she spoke aloud for him to hear.

"Look in the pond a mile behind my house, at the base of the granite pillar. Look when the sky is bright. Bring Amy with you. You'll see me, and you'll remember." She kissed him briefly on the lips and messed up his hair. "You're the most handsome boy in the world."

He smiled. "I'll remember that."

"I know you will," Julia said. She pressed his hand once again around her silver cord and gently closed his fingers, while she closed her own eyes. Suddenly, something *inside* her solar plexus snapped. Then she felt a strange sensation, of another hand closing around hers and lifting her up. She was reminded of when her mother used to take her by the hand as a child, at the beginning of their long, wonderful walks in the woods. Her mother would say, "Stay close to me, Julia. I wouldn't want to lose you."

"I wouldn't want to lose you, Mom."

Now Julia understood that was impossible.

Chapter Sixteen

AMY heard the siren as she pulled into the hospital parking lot. It was less than a mile behind her, which amazed her. After she had left Randy behind, she had driven like a madwoman. A black-and-white unit must have arrived at the liquor store within a minute of their stealing the cop car. Lieutenant Crawley was probably right on her tail.

Amy spotted her own car and parked beside it. She didn't even pause to close the police-car door when she jumped out; she was in too much of a hurry. Running toward the hospital, she hoped Julia had been denied entrance into intensive care. Yet she also knew that if Julia wanted in, Julia would get in.

A strange sight greeted Amy in the hallway outside intensive care. Sally Hanlon of how-old-are-you fame was filming two overweight nurses with Scott's camcorder. The nurses looked as if they were having the time of their lives. Amy ignored the whole group as she strode toward the door to intensive care. Unfortunately, one of the nurses saw her.

"Where are you going, young lady?" the nurse asked as Amy pulled the door open. The nurse hurried away from her place in the spotlight, while Sally lowered the camcorder and spoke quietly to the other woman. Amy recognized both nurses. They had been on duty the night before.

"You can't visit Scott without permission from his doctor," the first nurse said. "But I can tell you his condition hasn't changed since you were last here."

"I'm not here to see Scott," Amy said. "My friend Julia is in there with him. I've come to get her."

"No one's entered here since we came on duty at ten," the nurse said.

Amy glanced at Sally. "Are you sure?"

"I'm quite sure, young lady. Now, if you would please come back tomorrow."

Amy nodded to Sally. "What are you doing with that woman right there?"

The nurse flushed. "I believe that's no business of yours."

"How come she's filming you?" Amy insisted.

"That woman," the nurse said indignantly, "is a newsperson from the network. She's doing a documentary on the fine medical care we provide in this area."

Amy snorted. "That woman is a waitress who works in a coffee shop three miles from here." Amy reached for the door again. "Julia just used her to distract you so she could sneak in to see Scott."

The nurse grabbed her hand. "You're not allowed in there!"

Amy shook off the woman's hold. "And you're not allowed to desert your patients to stroke your vanity."

"How dare you!" the nurse hissed.

"I'll dare what I want. Now, either you let me enter right now or you get back in there and stop Julia."

The nurse wasn't given a chance to respond. A door a hundred feet behind them burst open. Julia's aunt, followed by Randy—in handcuffs—Lieutenant Crawley, and a second officer marched toward them. The nurse beside Amy put a hand to her mouth and said, "Oh, my."

Amy used the distraction to go into intensive care. The nurse was caught off guard—she had hardly begun to turn when the door was slammed in her face. Amy was pleased to see the door could be locked from the inside, and she wasted no time doing it. The pounding started right away, but Amy just walked away from it.

Amy took only a few seconds to reach Scott's bed. A few too many.

God, no. She did it.

Scott was sitting up in bed, the automatic respirator torn from his nose. Julia's head lay resting in his lap, and he was stroking her long red hair as Amy slowly shuffled up to them. He hardly looked up, his eyes glued to Julia's face, but he was the first one to speak.

"I found her this way when I woke up," he said.

"Is she . . ." Amy asked, unable to finish the sentence.

"Yes."

Amy sat on the side of the bed beside them. She was Witnessing a great miracle, something she had only read about in the Bible. But in the Bible, she thought, when Christ had raised Lazarus, it hadn't killed him. She wanted to be strong. She wanted to be happy. She began to cry, instead, tears that came from a place deep inside her where she had prayed she would never again feel such anguish. But Julia had sunk under the water once more, and there was no sign of her, and now there never would be. Amy closed her eyes and it was dark inside.

Amy didn't know how long she remained that way. The next thing she was conscious of was a bony hand on her shoulder. She looked up to find Julia's aunt standing beside her. The old woman could have been seeing Julia for the first time, for there was a glow of wonder in the aunt's mysterious eyes. But the wonder was soon dimmed and was replaced by great sorrow. The aunt glanced at Amy.

"Let me move close to her, child," the aunt said.

Amy stepped aside and let the aunt kneel beside Julia. The aunt put her right palm on Julia's forehead and closed her eyes. Amy became aware then that others were in the room: Randy, Sally, Lieutenant Crawley, his assistant officer, and the nurses. They stood at the foot of the bed and watched in silence. Scott caught Amy's eye.

"How could this happen?" he asked.

"I don't know," she whispered, watching the aunt. The old woman knelt perfectly rigidly for a couple of minutes before sucking in a sharp breath and sighing. She opened her strange eyes and stared off into the distance.

"I know nothing," she said.

"You don't know what killed her?" Scott asked.

"I do know that," the aunt said, shaking herself. She reached out and put her hand on Scott's bandaged head. This time she kept her eyes open as she studied his face. Another minute passed before she let him go.

"You are healed, young man. Leave this hospital tonight, before they make you sick again."

"That's out of the question," the nurse who had tried to stop Amy said from behind them. The aunt cast her a sharp glance.

"You stay out of this," the aunt told her. "You're a caretaker of illness. You know nothing of healing."

The nurse took a frightened step back and shut her prunelike lips. Scott gingerly touched the top of his head. He was confused. "I feel fine," he said. "But didn't I get shot?"

"You did," Amy said. She turned to the aunt. "Can't you do anything for Julia?"

The aunt shook her head. "I don't have her power."

"Why not?" Amy pleaded. "You can do so many other things."

The aunt reached down and caressed Julia's soft cheek. "Our little girl. We chased her here, and we chased her there. But she was always one step ahead of us, because none of us understood where she was going." The aunt looked at Amy. "Julia gave her life for your friend. I would give my life for Julia. But God will not take my life. It is not worth enough. Do you understand?"

"No," Amy said.

"Julia turned out to be greater than us all. You do understand, Amy. You knew all this before I did."

Amy could not bear the grief. "I wanted to be wrong," she moaned.

The aunt stood up. "My problem was different. I wanted to be right." She patted Amy on the back. "We've both learned something from Julia. Now we'll have to learn not to mourn her passing. Please come see me whenever you wish. We could talk together, you and I."

"Hold on just a second," Lieutenant Crawley said, barging forward. "I've listened to enough of this nonsense. What was Julia doing at the scene of the holdup? How did she know those hoodlums?"

The aunt stared at him. "You have no place here."

Lieutenant Crawley sneered. "I'm the one who brought you to this place. I shouldn't have stopped and picked you up. I bet you're all in this together."

"All in *what?*" the aunt asked, and the lieutenant was a fool not to note the deadly anger that had entered her voice. "Have you no shame? Can't you see this poor girl has just died?"

"Just committed suicide is more like it," Crawley said. He reached down and yanked the glass tube Amy had taken from Frank's garage out of Julia's back pocket. Julia's body continued to lay across Scott's lap, at an awkward angle, but not without grace. Even in death Julia was radiant—a light seemed to glow around her head. It was only then that Amy remembered that Julia had taken Frank's ice tube from her in the liquor store. Crawley sniffed the open end of it and chuckled. "She was a junkie, just like the guys who hit the liquor store." He glanced at his partner. "I told you they were all in this together."

"That tube does not belong to my niece," the aunt said softly. Crawley was oblivious to who he was mocking. Amy watched as the cold light glowed deep in the aunt's violet eyes. "You will put it away," she said. "You will leave this room. Then you will never speak ill of Julia again."

Crawley smiled thinly. "Are you threatening me?"

"I'm telling you," the aunt said.

"Or you will hurt me?" Crawley asked sarcastically, yet enjoying himself.

"No," the aunt said. "I won't hurt you. Your partner will." She glanced at the second policeman at the foot of the bed and held his eye for a moment. "Isn't that true, Officer?"

Crawley laughed. "Can you believe this, Adams?"

Adams drew his revolver and pointed it at Crawley. "Let's go, Lieutenant," he said flatly.

Crawley dropped the glass tube onto the floor, where it shattered. "What the hell," he gasped.

"If you don't do exactly as I said," the aunt went on. "He will kill you. Isn't that true, Officer?"

"Yes, ma'am," Adams said without emotion, cocking his revolver.

Crawley quickly put up his hands. "All right, I'm leaving." He stepped toward the exit, the two nurses stepping away from him.

"Hey, can I get these cuffs off?" Randy asked.

"Remove his cuffs," the aunt told Crawley just before he reached the door. Crawley hurried back inside, with Adams guarding him the whole time, and pulled out a key chain. Unfortunately, he was shaking so badly he was unable to get the proper key in the cuff lock. Randy ended up doing it for him. Crawley practically bolted from the room, and the nurses were not far behind him. Officer Adams—looking as if he had just done something he had dreamed of for years—gave the aunt a puzzled smile before leaving. Sally followed the whole proceeding in awe, but without fear. The aunt spoke to Randy.

"Take Julia's body out of this place," she said.

"Take her home. We'll have her cremated and spread her ashes in her favorite pond."

"Her pond," Scott whispered suddenly.

"What is it?" Amy asked.

Scott was thoughtful. "We'll have to see."

The aunt nodded sadly. "You will see." She touched Julia's sleeping face one last time. "You will see what I saw."

Epilogue

I⊤ was four days later that Amy and Scott sat beside
the pond and poured Julia's ashes into the clear water.
In those four days many things had happened.

Frank Truckwater was booked on multiple felony
accounts—attempted murder, theft, dealing in illegal
drugs. His case didn't look good. Yet he was young,
nineteen, and his lawyer predicted in the paper that
Frank would be out on parole before his twenty-fifth
birthday. Reading the article, Scott and Amy couldn't
decide if that was good or bad.

Stan Easton, Frank's accomplice, was only sixteen
years old, a minor, and the case against him was not as
strong, although the same article said he would be
doing plenty of time before his twentieth birthday
rolled around. But those years behind bars would not
start until he got out of the hospital. The doctors
thought Stan would walk again, but not well. In fact,
they said he was lucky to be alive. He had needed
numerous transfusions when he finally was brought
into the hospital.

Lieutenant Crawley resigned from the police force two days after Julia's death. Another article in the paper cited emotional stress as the reason for his hasty departure. Fellow officers—Adams among them—hinted in guarded remarks that Crawley was beginning to show signs of instability, citing recent paranoid delusions.

Jim Kovic was buried three days after being shot. The liquor-store owner, who was responsible for Jim's death, read a short prayer that he had specifically written for Jim's funeral. The man had not been charged with any crime, but he'd had to be helped from the church before he could complete the reading of his prayer. Amy and Scott had found the incident moving. Jim's parents had publicly forgiven the man, but he had been unable to forgive himself.

There was also a reading of Julia's will three days after her death. In it she left her house and the surrounding property to Amy and Scott. Because Julia was a minor at the time of her writing the will, Julia's aunt had the option of voiding the will. But she chose to let Julia's will stand.

Hiking to the pond with Julia's ashes—stored safely in a blue vase—Amy and Scott realized they were hiking across their own property. Neither had known that Mother Florence's land extended so deep into the woods. The morning was cold. Frost clung to the trees like blankets of white winter, although fall had scarcely begun. They walked slowly, and Scott with a limp. He said he felt fine, but Amy could see he had some catching up to do. His head scars were healing at a miraculous rate. Yet they were still tender, and Scott continued to wear head bandages.

The doctors at the hospital didn't know what to

make of Scott. They flipped when he discharged himself. One doctor, however, a friend of both the surgeon who had performed Scott's operation and Mother Florence, was not surprised by his miraculous recovery. When he heard of Julia's sudden collapse, he advised his colleagues to leave Scott as he was, without the benefit of further treatment. Amy suspected the doctor in question must have witnessed several of Mother Florence's miracles over the years.

Ice rimmed the pond as they knelt beside the water and set the vase on the ground beside them. They had come early—the sun was less than an hour above the horizon—but someone had been before them. Randy Classick was busy at work on a pine tree that stood twenty feet due east of the pond. So absorbed was he in his carving that they had to call to him to get his attention.

"So it is you!" Amy said, pleased. For the last two years she had been finding the faces whenever she walked in the woods. "I'm impressed."

Randy turned, startled. "I didn't hear you come up."

"We kept waiting for you to notice us," Scott said.

Randy stood directly in front of his work, trying to shield it with his body. "How's your head feeling?" he asked.

"A little hollow," Scott said.

"When will you be coming back to school?" Randy asked.

"Having trouble in chemistry?" Scott asked.

"Failed a test yesterday," Randy said. He nodded to the vase of ashes. "Is that what I think it is?"

Amy touched the vase. "This was her favorite spot."

"Yeah, I know," Randy said, and he had to swallow. He looked down at the knife in his hand.

"Can we see it?" Scott asked.

"What?" Randy asked innocently.

"I bet it's Julia," Amy said.

Randy reluctantly stepped aside. The carving was at the level Julia's face would have been, and it was exquisite. Besides being closest to the pond, the pine Randy had chosen for his masterpiece was big and old. The bark was unusually thick and dry, which had given him a fine base for detail. He had cast Julia in a happy light—not with a huge grin, but with the faint, knowing smile that had been her trademark. The flow of her hair over the bark was a wonder—it looked as if the wood were blowing in the wind. Amy couldn't get over how realistic it was. She did note that Randy had a photograph tucked in the pocket of his jacket, which she would have wagered was of Julia.

"I just came to put a few finishing touches on it," Randy said, almost apologetically. "I've been working on it for the last couple of days." He nodded to the vase again. "But if you guys want to be alone, I don't mind. I can come back later."

"No. Stay," Amy said, patting the ground beside her. "I'm sure Julia would want you here."

"What are we going to do?" Randy asked self-consciously as he walked over and joined them on the cold grass. Amy half wished they had brought a blanket, yet there was also something nice about the feel of the earth so close to their skin. Randy added, "I don't know any prayers, if that's what you're going to say. The minister at my parents' church told me when I was twelve years old not to come back until I learned to fear God."

221

"Why did he tell you that?" Scott asked.

"I think it was the Walkman I used to wear to church," Randy said.

"We're not going to pray normal prayers," Amy said. "Scott?"

Now it was Scott's turn to appear self-conscious, which was perhaps a first for him. "I have this weird idea," he said. "I don't know where I got it. But I think that if we pour Julia's ashes in this water, and let them sink down, and look in the water with the sunlight on it, we'll see something."

"What?" Randy asked.

"I don't know," Scott said.

"Have you had any other weird ideas since you got shot in the head?" Randy asked.

"Randy," Amy said, "you have to be respectful at a time like this."

"I'm trying." Randy eyed the vase uneasily. "What's left of her isn't gross or anything, is it?"

"No," Scott said, picking up the vase. He looked at it silently for a moment. "It's beautiful." He handed the vase to Amy. "You were her best friend. You do it."

"OK," Amy said. She unplugged the cork from the top of the vase and began to sprinkle the ashes lightly on the pond's surface. Then she began to hum softly, a song she didn't know the words to. She thought it was a song Mother Florence had sung when they walked together, but she couldn't be sure. It just came to her out of nowhere. To either side of her, she noticed Randy and Scott had closed their eyes. She closed hers. She finished sprinkling the ashes and briefly submerged the vase, pouring the water back into the pond, moving by feel alone. Setting the vase by her side, she sat with her own eyes closed for several minutes. All the time she was aware of her friends beside her, but she was unaware of their breathing, or even her own. The three of them were so settled, they could have been figures carved in the trees. Finally, Scott spoke.

"Let's open our eyes and look in the water," he said softly.

Amy's eyes felt remarkably heavy, and she opened them with some difficulty. As she peered into the pond, however, a peculiar lightness spread through her limbs and flowed into her head. It was like a magnetic current that possessed the power to transform flesh and blood into something finer, more permanent. A wave of silent exhilaration swept over her right then, and she realized that all the ashes were gone, absorbed by the pond, a miracle in itself. Not even the tiniest particle floated on the mirrored surface. Yes, Amy understood; it was a mirror, of course. That was why Julia had spent so much time peering into its depths—to see things inside herself, things of another world, another time.

Julia's giving us her vision now.

Later, Amy was never to know for sure if what she saw right then was her imagination or if it was real. Yet if it was a dream, then the three of them shared it in exact detail.

Julia was swimming from the center of the lake where Scott and Julia had almost drowned, swimming to the shore, to a place where her mother stood waiting. The sun shone brilliantly on the two of them, and Julia had only to cross the width of the sandy shore and take her mother's hand to be dry. Amy watched as they turned and walked into the woods, following them along a narrow shaded path that led to where Randy and Scott and she now sat, beside the pond. But Julia and her mother did not pause to look in the water; at least not right away. They circled behind the granite hill that stood beside the pond and scaled to the top, moving with springy steps that knew nothing of gravity. At the peak, they clasped their hands together once more and stared down at the pond as the morning sun shone on its delicate surface.

I'm seeing through her eyes.

It was true—for Amy could see herself sitting on the grass beside Randy and Scott. Amy was right there with Julia when Julia turned to her mother and asked, "Do you think they can see us?"

Mother Florence nodded. "They see the sun." Then she smiled at her daughter. "Come, it's time to step into the sky."

Julia smiled. "And fly higher than the highest bird?"

"Yes," Mother Florence said.

Together they stepped off the peak. Yet they didn't fall, not that Amy could see. They simply vanished. Amy jerked her head up, away from her vision on the water. They all did.

But there was nothing there.

"Weird," Randy whispered.

Amy looked at him. "You saw them?" she asked.

"I saw something," Randy said, lowering his gaze back to the pond.

"How about you, Scott?" Amy asked.

Scott nodded and pointed to Randy's carving in the tree. The sun had moved behind Julia's face, behind the tree, and the morning rays glowed at the edges of the bark like flames. Amy recalled Mother Florence's words of a moment ago and knew them to be true. It was blinding to look at the carving. Julia had merged in the sun, in this world and the next.

"I remember she came to me at the hospital," Scott said.

"What did she say?" Amy asked.

"That you and I should go to Tahiti together," Scott said.

"I believe it," she said.

"I can carve Jim on the tree beside her tree," Randy suggested. "If you don't mind, Amy?"

Amy looked at the tree and smiled. "I don't mind."

About the Author

CHRISTOPHER PIKE was born in Brooklyn, New York, but grew up in Los Angeles, where he lives to this day. Prior to becoming a writer, he worked in a factory, painted houses, and programmed computers. His hobbies include astronomy, meditating, running, playing with his nieces and nephews, and making sure his books are prominently displayed in local bookstores. Christopher Pike is the author of forty teen thrillers available from Archway Paperbacks and Pocket Pulse.

Christopher Pike

DARK SECRETS™
by Elizabeth Chandler

Who is Megan? She's about to find out....
#1: Legacy of Lies

Megan thought she knew who she was.

Until she came to Grandmother's house.

Until she met Matt, who angered and attracted her as no boy ever had before.

Then she began having dreams again, of a life she never lived, a love she never

knew...a secret that threatened to drive her to the grave.

Home is where the horror is....
#2: Don't Tell

Lauren is coming home, eight years after her mother's mysterious drowning. They said

it was an accident. But the tabloids screamed murder. Aunt Jule was her only refuge,

the beloved second mother she's returning to see. But first Lauren stops at Wisteria's

annual street festival and meets Nick, a tease, a flirt, and a childhood playmate.

The day is almost perfect—until she realizes she's being watched.

A series of nasty "accidents" makes Lauren realize someone wants her dead.

And this time there's no place to run....

Archway Paperbacks
Published by Pocket Books

William Corlett's

THE MAGICIAN'S HOUSE QUARTET

Thirteen-year-old William Constant and his two younger sisters, Mary
and Alice, have come to ancient, mysterious Golden House in Wales for
the holidays. Their lives will never be the same once they enter the
Magician's House—and discover their destiny.

THE STEPS UP THE CHIMNEY
What evil lurks in Golden House? The children know....

William knew something was wrong from the moment they arrived at
the railroad station on the border of Wales. First came the stranger who
said his name was Steven. "Remember me," he said. Then he vanished.
By the time they reached Golden House, even Mary and Alice felt something odd. Who—or what—are the strange animals...a fox, a dog, an
owl...that seem to be able to read their minds? Why is it that sometimes
the children even see out of the eyes of the animals and hear with their
ears? And what is that prickling sensation pulling them toward the
secret steps up the chimney? Nothing can stop them as they are drawn
deep into the old house, into the realm of the Magician.

THE DOOR IN THE TREE
It's even more dangerous when the magic is real....

It's vacation again—time for William, Mary, and Alice to return to Golden
House. They've made a solemn vow not to speak of anything that happened on their last visit to Uncle Jack's home. Was the magic real? It
seems like a dream to William and Mary. Only Alice knows the secret of
magic: believing. It is Alice who discovers the Dark and Dreadful Path,
Alice who is irresistibly drawn into the ancient yew tree. And it is Alice
who finds the door in the tree—leading to the secret hiding place of the
Magician. *It wasn't a dream!*

Soon they've become the Magician's students, led by the kestrel, the
badgers, and the dog into the most perilous assignment of all....

And coming in the fall of 2001:
THE TUNNEL BEHIND THE WATERFALL
THE BRIDGE IN THE CLOUDS

Available from Archway Paperbacks
Published by Pocket Books

3044

They're real,
and they're here...

When Jack Dwyer's best friend
Artie is murdered, he is devastated.
But his world is turned upside down
when Artie emerges from the ghostlands
to bring him a warning.

With his dead friend's guidance,
Jack learns of the Prowlers. They
move from city to city, preying on
humans until they are close to being
exposed, then they move on.

Jack wants revenge. But even as he
hunts the Prowlers, he marks himself—
and all of his loved ones—as prey.

Don't miss the exciting
new series from

BESTSELLING AUTHOR
CHRISTOPHER GOLDEN!

PROWLERS

POCKET
PULSE

PUBLISHED BY POCKET BOOKS   3083